Just Over Broke

Miles Atwell

2QT (Publishing) Ltd

First Edition published 2022 by
2QT Limited (Publishing)
Settle, N. Yorkshire

Cover image: iStock by Getty Images
Back image: shutterstock.com

Printed by IngramSpark

A CIP catalogue record for this book is available
from the British Library

ISBN 978-1-914083-40-2

Acknowledgements

A massive thank you to Joseph Turner, Katherine Blessan and Emma Alison for all your help in beta and proofreading. *Just Over Broke* would still be a random Word Doc that even the Cloud wouldn't keep hold of if it were not for your efforts.

Thanks also to the staff at 2QT for all their help in getting this ten-year project completed at last.

One

The five-foot-tall Dalmatian strode confidently onto the stage to much applause. It gyrated eagerly in front of the 600-strong audience as if the person inside the suit were possessed by the spirit of a dead dancer. There were shrieks and cheers from the overexcited audience as the giant dog strutted to one end of the floodlit stage and threw its great paws in the air to wave at the tables full of swinging dicks. Its dance back to the centre of the stage was less enthusiastic, and Rick presumed the occupant was not quite as young as the many gathered employees.

If the dog wasn't enough to make Rick roll his eyes, then the sudden and very violent blast of hardcore rave music certainly was. He had to be careful he didn't show his emotions in case his team leader witnessed them and accused him of looking too sarcastic.

The Dalmatian stopped dancing after a few minutes and took an exhausted bow. At that moment the music cut out. Rick was relieved his head no longer felt like a prison van being thumped by self-righteous protestors.

'Ladies and gentlemen, welcome to the 2009 Mercury Group Sales and Marketing Awards ceremony! Please welcome to the stage Tessa Jansen and Paul Jackson,' a voice boomed over the PA system, sending vibrations through everyone's eardrums.

The appearance of the two business leaders was like footage of The Beatles disembarking a plane in England. The whole room erupted again with cheering and shouting. People jumped up and down on their chairs. So much for health and safety. Eventually everyone calmed down and let the two presenters speak.

Grabbing the mic from its stand, a tall middle-aged woman playfully shoved her companion away before addressing her adoring audience. 'It's amazing to see you all here today. Well done for not getting lost, Lee,' Jansen said.

Everyone turned towards the table where Lee and the Sheffield office were sitting, pointing and laughing like schoolchildren at them.

Jansen clipped the mic back into the stand and made a great show of allowing Jackson the space to take the floor.

'Thanks for letting me speak, Tessa. Yes, it really is great to be here today. There are a lot of very good businessmen and women in this room, and we want to reward all your incredibly hard work.' His slur on the 'yes' suggested he'd hit the complementary drinks table before his colleagues.

The conference dragged on, with many people winning the coveted awards. Rick felt like he was watching an endless graduation ceremony as salesperson after salesperson went up to collect certificates and gift vouchers. Once that had finished, Tessa Jansen stood up to kick start the speeches.

'A lot of people ask me why I wanted to start my own business. Most of us have a different reason for it. Some of us like the prestige it gives, some want to escape from the normal working world, some want to better themselves – and we all want to make money.' There were murmurs of agreement with the last comment from around the room.

'I have another very specific reason. Twelve years ago, I became a mum. Everyone told me I couldn't be a successful businesswoman and bring up a child. Well, I have become a very successful businesswoman and I now bring up two children. Now, I'm not just telling you that to show off. The reason I mention my two girls is that they motivate me. I did well at my job because I was determined that they would not be sent to a state school. I want them to have the best and that means paying for private education.'

A look of victory was stamped across her face, the type of look you would get from a lottery winner going into work one last time to gloat at their unlucky ex-colleagues.

The room was full of nodding heads. Hardly anyone in the room had gone to public school, yet they still seemed to think that sending their kids to state school was like shipping them off to Borstal.

Later, Paul Jackson made an equally infuriating speech. 'We do a very difficult job and not many people like us,' was the only thing he said that Rick agreed with.

'There's a quote I heard that sums up my position and how I overcame everyone's put-downs. It was by Mahatma Gandhi. "First they ignore you, then they ridicule you, then they fight you, then you win." Make sure you write that down and remember it, because quotes like that inspired me to get to where I am today.'

Rick noticed with annoyance that many in the room were actually making notes. At least the speech was forgivably short; after all, Jackson needed to get back to the bar.

The same pounding music built up after the speech and the dog took its rightful place on the stage. Yet again the crowd went wild. Rick looked at the excited people around him who would no doubt spend the next morning talking about what a 'legendary' evening it had been.

The young man sitting next to him leaned over and shouted over the noise, 'Who do you think the dog is?'

Rick sighed and shouted back, 'I don't know, some mad man,' and got up to leave.

Having been stuck for two hours in the long-windedly-titled Manchester Central Convention Complex, Rick was hot. He didn't fancy staying for the congratulations, high-fiving and celebratory drinks that would soon run out. He'd go to The Earl instead.

After manoeuvring himself past several dancing sales reps, he made it to the exit. He heaved a sigh of relief as he left the venue through its large main entrance and was hit by the freezing night air.

o-• •-o

The Earl had once been an Edwardian mill-owner's house. It stood in dismal solitude in the middle of a large garden, thick ivy vines clinging around the door as though the building had grown a rather uneven green goatee beard. Naturally this garden was now a beer garden, where in summer the masses crowded around picnic tables to smoke, drink cold beer and generally be astonished by the presence of a fiery ball in the sky.

Rick knew The Earl better as his regular watering hole and had arranged to meet his flatmate Callum there. A torrential downpour started whilst he walked from the bus stop to the pub, and he hurried in, barely taking time to read the chalk noticeboard that proudly proclaimed it was tribute night.

Once inside, he was hit by the familiar smell of ale soaking into carpet and the sight of a less-than-busy taproom. In the corner The Whom were already packing up, obviously not having raised the roof. The few regulars who remained were either attempting to chat up the illegally employed seventeen-year-old barmaid, who looked more terrified than disgusted by them, or working the fruit machines with the concentration and skills of Bletchley Park code breakers.

Callum had found them a table in the corner and had a pint of lager waiting for Rick. He wore ripped jeans and a T-shirt so faded that its once-amusing slogan had become illegible. He lifted his hand and gave a mock royal wave.

Rick approached the table and bowed before hanging his wet coat over the back of the chair. The water drips were the closest the maroon-and-orange carpet had ever been to a wash. He sat down and leaned back into the damp hood, wetting his suit jacket. Smooth. 'How was the band?' he asked.

'Delightfully awful. But at least they weren't as bad as The Vinyl Solution.'

Rick had met Callum in the student bar at Manchester Metropolitan University ten years earlier, when they had been attempting lives of scholarly leisure. They had been invited there by mutual friends with whom neither had stayed in touch. Callum had suggested a game of knockout pool where each time a player potted a ball his opponent had to shout the childish slang word for female genitals very loudly. Rick had been a tournament-winning pool and snooker player in his teenage years and had beaten Callum in each game. Naturally, the two had become friends.

'How was the conference?' Callum asked.

'There was a giant dog.'

'Of course there was.'

'It danced on the stage,' Rick said without humour.

Callum had become used to Rick's stories of workplace shenanigans and wouldn't have been shocked to hear that the Prime Minister of Legoland had come on stage and bitten the head off a rhino.

'Job still bollocks then?' Callum ventured, knowing full well it was a sore subject.

'A bit of an understatement. It's not just the stupid conferences or my team leader, who, by the way, said last week that I wasn't putting in enough effort. I mean how can I talk to customers with a door slammed in my face?' Rick ranted, not for the first time.

'Your work's weird. It sounds like everyone there gets turned on by selling. They probably treat the sales bible like porn. You're the normal one, remember,' Callum reassured him.

'I know, I just don't feel like it.' The first pint was going down quickly.

'There's a very simple solution to that problem, mate. You should do what you've been saying you want to do for the last year.' Callum sounded slightly more serious this time.

'I keep wanting to quit, but it's very hard at the moment. You can't just leave your job during a recession and expect to find another one straight away.' It was a thought that had plagued Rick for some time.

'You have to do it. This job is turning you into a cynical and depressed old fart twenty years too early. I don't understand why you can't just go into your MD's office and tell him how you feel.' Callum decided this was the time to get in another round and fled to the bar before Rick could point out that the round was his.

Rick sat silently, thinking where to take the conversation next. 'Have I ever told you about my managing director, Daniel McNabb?' he asked as Callum returned with two fresh pints.

'McNabb? Yeah, I remember the name. Scottish bloke who everyone's in love with?'

'Everyone in the Mercury Group, yes. But it's not hard to see why. He really does offer us a lot of encouragement, even the minions like me. The problem is, it's hard to tell him that I don't like doing what we do and don't want to be part of his company,' Rick admitted.

'You aren't doing yourself any favours by carrying

on like this. Can you at least try to talk to him about it? If he's that understanding, he'll hear you out. Then you can decide what to do next.'

'You're right,' Rick agreed. 'I have to do it. I probably *will* do it.'

'There's that enthusiasm I love so much. Obviously, if you do quit make sure you get another job straight after – we've still got rent to pay,' Callum pointed out.

They continued drinking for some time until a shocked gasp came from the bar, catching the attention of the few remaining patrons. The barmaid looked ready to slap a large sweaty man who was guffawing at his own comment. Another of the other regulars was laughing at them both.

'Not that I don't want to carry on chatting to you, mate, but I feel like Sara needs saving from those gargoyles.' Callum smiled cheekily and looked over at the barmaid.

'It's lucky you only look about twelve otherwise people might think making a move on her was very dodgy.' Callum was ten years the girl's senior and Rick knew he'd been waiting for this moment for a long time. All those hours spent in the gym inflating and then sculpting his body were about to pay off.

'I need an early night anyway,' Rick said, finishing his drink. He stepped outside into the unrelenting rain and made a dash for the nearest bus stop.

Two

When Rick awoke, he couldn't remember what time he had returned from The Earl. As he heaved his head off the pillow pain split his brain in two, causing his head to drop back onto its feathered crash mat. He lay there for some time, not wanting to move, before eventually sliding out of bed and onto the carpeted floor. He dragged himself up using the side of the bed and stumbled into the bathroom, where his stomach attempted to escape through his mouth and into the toilet. He stood retching for a few minutes, not much coming out.

A splash of cold water in the face didn't make him feel much better. He lifted his head to look at the mirror and noticed how his pale skin looked even more colourless than usual and his face was not as thin as it used to be.

He wondered how so few pints had done so much damage. In years gone by, he had drunk like a thirsty fish and rarely felt as bad as he did now. His contemplation was interrupted by a big stomach churn, and his head went back over the bog. This time his stomach lining decided to join in with the fun.

After cleaning himself up, Rick dressed in his usual plain black suit and unimaginative tie. It was often said that he looked like an undertaker, a comment to which he took no offence.

Despite feeling delicate, he decided to attempt breakfast. After managing only two mouthfuls of toast, a glass of cloudy water and some paracetamol, he decided he had best head to work. No sound could be heard from Callum's room, and Rick was unsure how successfully his friend's night had ended.

The flat was in a modern, but basic, tower block a few miles from the centre of Manchester. Rick and Callum had moved there after leaving university. It suited their none-too-extravagant tastes, and it was in an area that the estate agent described as 'characterful'. The strong herbal smells that hit Rick's nostrils at the bus stop suggested that some of the local characters had enjoyed their night out, too.

On any morning Manchester city centre was murder, but today it was mass homicide. Rick didn't start work until 10.30am, yet every weekday he found himself navigating around dawdlers who seemed to have nothing to do. After disembarking from the bus, he knew he'd have to resort to gentle and polite shoving to get away from the kerb, cross the concourse and make it to the bus station's exit.

This, he also knew, would have to be done quickly enough to avoid being decapitated by the wing mirror of his bus as it pulled off.

In the station, he was met by a barrage of noise: snippets of conversations, the wheels of suitcases on the lino floor, the cracking of dozens of pigeon's wings as they scattered from various storeys of the building.

He tried to cross the large main entrance of the bus station, but the mass of commuters made it feel like he was swimming against a river of bodies. After several nudges, knocks and muttered apologies, he triumphantly reached the dry land of the exit gasping for breath.

He ambled through the city centre, dodging between screeching trams and the public. The early-morning drinkers were out, walking tall and straight for the first few hours of the day. The sound of acoustic guitars playing a funky version of 'Hotel California' announced that unusually talented buskers were in town. They were the type of tie-dyed hippies who looked like they were ready for a ban-the-bomb march. One of them, the one with the mightiest beard and therefore their leader, turned to look directly at Rick and shouted, 'But you can never leave,' a line that got stuck on repeat in Rick's head as he was confronted by the building in which he worked.

The tower block was nine floors high and looked

as modern as it did mundane. The whole outer surface was made of glass so that passers-by could look right into the various businesses that were housed within. As he approached, Rick felt like a voyeur for commerce watching the shirt-and-tie-clad workers carrying files between desks. Scurrying across the main road, Rick thought he saw a frustrated man slam his fist down on his desk.

For two years Rick had been employed by a company called Gold Force, which was part of the larger Mercury Group that was pretentiously named after the Roman god of commerce. Their main client was the gas and electricity supplier N-ergise. It was Rick's job to try and convince people to switch to them.

'You're not the most persuasive man in the world,' had been his team leader's first professional observation. Sadly Rick couldn't use lethal force or threats on potential customers, so he rarely benefitted from the ten percent commission that all sales reps were entitled to.

He entered the building and ascended the zigzagging staircase to the second floor where Gold Force was based. The large central office was buzzing with activity. The happy workers were young and mostly good looking. As Rick entered, attempting to look as sober as he could, most of them were laughing or gesticulating enthusiastically whilst sharing stories about their nights out. Many had arrived earlier than necessary to try and talk to people more important than themselves. Rick never arrived earlier than he had to.

The office was quite basic considering the amount of money generated there. It was free of PCs, and it wasn't necessary for the reps to have their own desks, so it was mostly clear save for several whiteboards dotted around. In front of these stood energetic salespeople writing massive words of encouragement for their colleagues and discussing the best ways to sell.

Posters were stuck on some of the surrounding windows with those annoying little sayings that are supposed to inspire people, slogans like *You always miss 100% of the shots you don't take* printed below a picture of a basketball net.

'Rick, how are you, man?' Saj, one of the reps, walked over and shook Rick's hand firmly.

'Not too bad, mate. Did you work over the weekend?' Rick thought he'd avoid mentioning the conference; anyway, any gossip would soon be dispersed around the room like toxic gas.

'Yeah, it was sound! You really missed out. Time and a half!' Saj said, playfully jab-crossing Rick's arm.

Rick hid his annoyance well. 'You know how strongly I feel on the matter of working weekends. Just because God waited six days before He had a rest doesn't mean I'm working Saturdays.'

Saj straightened up from his boxer stance. 'I'd be a bit more careful saying stuff like that if I was you, man,' he said quietly.

Rick had uttered the great blasphemy of a negative comment. Usually if someone complained, the neg-head in question would have to find a positive angle on the situation.

'Are you all ready to make some cash?' A booming voice suddenly drowned out the noise of chatting. It was Dylan, Rick's team leader.

Everyone in the room turned to face him. Sixty voices all screamed back 'Yes!'. He moved to the centre of the room, all eyes upon him.

'I can't hear you. I said are you all ready to make some cash?!!!' Despite sounding like a nineties' game-show host, Dylan was dressed in the expensive suit of a boardroom executive; it had evidently been tailored to fit his sleek, six-foot body. He was the best-dressed man in the room and he knew it.

The room cheered again, this time so loudly that Rick was sure that a deaf old man in Stockport would hear them. Every morning, one of the eight team leaders would conduct a meeting. There was a lot of talk about sales and how much money certain people had made and how many more cities they had taken over. Rick generally tuned out during these bits.

'So, what do you think the most important thing

is when selling N-ergise?' Dylan asked.

Rick sighed. If only that were a rhetorical question.

'Being confident about the product,' a woman said.

'Yes, that's important, but what's the *most* important thing?' Dylan persisted.

'Making sure they make you a cup of tea when they let you in,' a man in his forties, suggested to much laughter.

'Yeah, nice one. But seriously, the answer I'm looking for is good customer-service skills.' Dylan turned round on the spot so he could see all the faces nodding in agreement.

'Yes, but knowing the product is also very important, isn't it?' the same woman asked.

Looking exasperated, Dylan turned to her. He reached into his pocket. 'Get your car keys out.' He pulled out his own and stared straight into the woman's eyes. She looked very confused and said nothing. 'What car do you drive? Do you think it cost more than mine?' Dylan asked her.

Rick knew his colleagues would quietly watch this rebuke and think nothing of it.

'I haven't got one, but I was just trying to say...' the woman started, but Dylan wouldn't let her finish.

'Exactly! I've made a lot of money doing this. Trust me – it's good customer-service skills. I'm trying to help you to get rich. Do you understand?' This time he smiled as he questioned her. The woman nodded.

What followed was a long speech about making yourself as appealing as you could to the customer, not an easy task for someone like Dylan.

'Show of hands. How many of you are gonna to make mega-bucks today?' He looked expectantly round the room. Most put their hands up, even Rick. 'I should see every hand up right now. We work in sales and we are fucking good at making money, right?'

Everyone cheered.

'Here are some other things to get you excited. There are day trips!' Dylan continued.

Everyone cheered.

'There are road trips!'

Everyone cheered.

'There are bonuses!'

Everyone cheered.

'There are trips paintballing and zorbing!'

Two cheers for those.

'So, everyone get out onto those streets and make as many sales as you can. There is no upper limit,' he finished.

Inwardly, Rick cheered.

Dylan's team of eight gathered together at one end of the office so their leader could do a quick roll-call before unleashing them onto an unsuspecting suburb of the city. As people came

17

and went frequently from Gold Force, the team was not always the same and Rick only recognised four of the present group. Eric and Carla had been in the team longer than he had, although he didn't know either of them very well. Apart from Dylan, the only other member of the team that Rick knew anything about was Christine. He liked Christine; she was one of his few colleagues that he didn't want to punch in the face.

Christine had been born and raised in Kenya to a native mother and an ex-Etonian father. He was a British diplomat who had moved the family back to London when Christine was eleven years old. That gave her an Estuary English accent, which had led to her being labelled 'a posh southerner' when she arrived in Manchester at twenty-two and fell in love with the place.

Rick sneaked up behind her in the lobby and grabbed her shoulders, causing a much louder screech than he had anticipated. He also hadn't anticipated Christine dropping her lunchbox, nor the Tupperware lid detaching from it on impact with the floor. As guffawing broke out from the surrounding reps, Rick scrambled about on all fours grabbing celery sticks and cherry tomatoes.

'Well, I suppose it makes a change from your usual stalking,' she said playfully as he handed the box back to her.

'I don't know what you're talking about. I just

happen to go to the same pedicurist as you,' Rick replied.

'Oh, I'm not talking about that. Every time I come to work, you're here. It's almost as if there's a *reason* for you being here,' she laughed.

'Come on, you two. The bus sets off in five and we have to get to the field.' Dylan was always desperate to get to the field. In any other workplace he'd be a complete nerd but, in the exciting world of direct sales, men like him were rock stars.

Whilst the team waited at the bus stop, Eric started bobbing around on his toes, mentally preparing himself for the day ahead. The others were messing around with their phones, sending messages to their partners and friends about what they'd be doing when they finally got home. It was a long way off.

Just before the bus pulled up, Rick turned to Christine. 'One thing still confuses me,' he told her.

'Really? What's that?'

'What the fuck is zorbing?'

∘━● ●━∘

Rick and Christine were sitting at the back of the bus, Rick laughing whilst Christine tried to describe the finer points of a sport where you rolled down a hill. He wished that this part of the day lasted longer, or that they didn't have to get off the bus at all but could be driven around in circles all day.

Going into the field was the main part of the job; it was where the selling of N-ergise happened. There were some parts of it Rick liked. It kept him outdoors and gave him some of the only exercise his steadily bulging body so desperately needed. However, it also meant having to meet potential customers, which was rarely fun.

After disembarking, Dylan would usually find a place of interest for a starting point, often a shop or pub car park. Being a military enthusiast, Dylan would normally call it something like an 'RV point' or an 'HQ'. They would disperse from this secure location with a list of about ninety houses to work with.

Then came the bit everyone loved – selling! Or 'doorbell testing', as Rick called it. The day was spent traipsing up and down the mean streets of suburban Manchester trying to talk people into changing how they paid their energy bills.

'Remember, all the pipes and wires stay the same. The only difference is the logo on the top of the bill,' was one of the humiliating phrases they'd been taught to say.

They were also encouraged to tell those little white sales lies to convince people they could make big savings, although whenever a representative from N-Ergise visited the office these persuasion techniques were suddenly discouraged by the team leaders during pitch practice.

The area Dylan had chosen for the RV point was outside a large Asda at the end of a retail park. Rick looked around and felt like it was Groundhog Day again. He liked Manchester as a city but was sick of having to work the suburbs where there was so little character and everything ended up looking the same. The houses were well-kept and the area appeared pleasing to the eye, but you got the feeling that nobody cared about it. In a similar way, nobody else in the team cared and only saw it as a place to cash in. They couldn't give a toss if the supermarket was a carbon copy of the one five miles away that they were near last Monday.

'This is the most central location in our area. I've looked on the GPS and it's easily the best place.' Dylan waved his phone around just in case there was anyone present who didn't realise that was where his GPS was.

'Right, let's get started.' Eric was nearly shrieking with excitement.

'Enthusiastic! Good man.' Dylan sounded impressed. He positioned himself in front of his troops, like a suit-clad Alexander the Great. 'Listen, guys. This is a very middle-class area. I love these places. The people here are shit scared of their neighbours getting something they haven't got. Remember, they are all sheep.' He sounded completely confident; he was about to make a lot of money.

They went their separate ways and started looking for houses with signs of life.

o—• •—o

Two no answers, one 'bugger off' and three 'come back later when we're definitely, honestly, going to be in'. And it was only midday. Rick still had eighty-one doors on his list. What thrills were still in store?

The next house was number nineteen. It looked just like number seventeen: three floors of sandblasted similarity. It had a long drive running alongside a garden that seemed to be used as a dumping ground for various expensive outdoor toys. Rick stepped over a ride-on fire engine that had been left outside the front door.

He hesitated before reaching for the bell, composing himself. Ding dong. Original.

The door was opened slowly by a woman who had a phone in one hand and two unruly toddlers running around her legs.

'Hello,' Rick began. 'Sorry to bother you, it's just a quick call about your gas and electric.' He held up his N-ergise ID in case she didn't get the point.

'Yeah, it's alright love, someone's at the door. I won't be a second,' the woman said down the phone in a slight Scouse accent.

'I'm just here to let you know that you can save up

22

to £200 a year on your energy bills with N-ergise. If you don't mind me asking, how do you pay your energy bills?' Rick pressed on, unperturbed by having less than her full attention.

'Look, my bills are already taken care of. I can't change anything. Aye, get off!' she shouted at her son, who had grabbed her thigh with both hands and was squeezing hard.

Rick considered walking away but, as he had rung her doorbell, it would seem rude.

'No, not you, love. Toby's just getting too clingy,' she carried on down the phone, looking at Rick impatiently.

'So, are you on a meter?' Rick asked.

'No, I'm on the phone.'

He had to hand it to her, that was a good one even if it pissed him off. 'You look busy at the moment. Maybe I'll come back some other time.' Rick started to edge backwards and almost tripped over the fire engine. The woman rolled her eyes and shut the door.

Back on the streets, and with one more door ticked off, Rick's head was still throbbing. He wished there was somewhere nearby he could hide for a bit, but there was nothing but cloned houses on his patch. He considered going back to Asda to waste an hour or so looking at the magazines and DVDs, but he'd probably be spotted by Dylan.

Asda wasn't as busy as Rick had anticipated, which

suited him fine and allowed him some breathing space. He stood in one aisle for around twenty minutes, flicking through National Geographic, before hunger got the better of him and he chose a wrap out of one of the fridges. He didn't rush as he made his way to the checkout and paid.

When he emerged from the store, he unwrapped the wrap and bit into it. At that exact moment, his phone went off. *Great timing, Dylan*; only his team leader could ring at such an inconvenient moment.

As Rick fished his phone out of his pocket, the bottom of the wrap split and he received a lovely blob of Cajun sauce on his shirt. Cursing himself for leaving his jacket unbuttoned, he almost answered the phone by calling Dylan a clumsy tit. 'Hi,' he managed instead.

'Hi. Are you getting on okay?' Dylan asked.

'Not bad. The usual, really,' Rick said, even though the usual was bad and he knew Dylan was well aware of that.

'Okay. Well, keep going. The team are going to RV one more time before end of play at around 6.30pm.'

'Okay, see you then.' Rick hung up. He wasn't looking forward to the meeting, or RV, or whatever Dylan wanted to think of it as. He knew the rest of the team would have had an amazing day and would all be deciding what to spend their riches on.

The day hadn't gone well and, after finishing work, Rick made his way home as quickly as he could. He took a seat on the top deck of the bus to try and put as much distance as he could between himself and his fellow commuters.

Things had to change. He'd known that for some time, but now he felt he needed to make a move soon before he became too familiar with his underachieving life. The idea of quitting work yet again tried to break the defensive wall of his indecisiveness. It banged on the portcullis repeatedly until he could ignore it no longer, but he knew he wasn't qualified to do much else. His degree in English Literature wouldn't help, and all his work experience came courtesy of dead-end retail jobs. Quitting wouldn't be as easy as it sounded.

There might be one light at the end of the tunnel, though: Dylan. Rick knew Dylan had complained to McNabb about his performance and how little money Rick had made Gold Force over the last few months. Dylan could even turn out to be an unlikely saviour.

However, the crestfallen look on Daniel McNabb's face when he realised how much misplaced faith he'd wasted on Rick was one Rick never wanted to witness; it made him cringe.

As Rick arrived home, he was still no nearer to making a decision about his job and he decided to have an early night.

Three

The morning began earlier than usual for Rick and with a bit more optimism. Whilst he made his tea and toast, he thought about the day ahead and weighed up his options:

Option 1: Go to work as normal and hope that my recent piss-poor performance results in employment termination.

Option 2: Arrive at work early, walk into McNabb's office and tell him I want to leave Gold Force and find another job.

Option 3: Do exactly the same thing I've done for the last year – go to work as normal and tolerate the madness.

The right option was obvious, yet every time Rick thought about it he pictured that look of disappointment on McNabb's face. McNabb might even be offended that Rick hadn't said something earlier.

Callum was still in bed when he slipped out of the flat around 8am. Rick didn't know what time his flatmate would rise – in fact, he didn't even know what he did for a living. Callum seemed to change his job every week and it was impossible to keep up with where he actually worked.

Rick walked to the bus stop, trying to inspire confidence within himself as he went, convinced that he could get out. It would be simple – just one little meeting with McNabb and his career could be euthanised.

The key to it all, he realised, was timing. McNabb was always the first to arrive and the last to leave the office. He occasionally took the lead with the morning meetings instead of the team leaders. If it was one of those mornings, Rick figured that he could catch McNabb before the meeting started. It was then a simple matter of convincing the boss that the company no longer needed dead weight. Surely lack of sales plus general lack of enthusiasm equalled termination?

The bus arrived late and Rick flashed his pass with Ninja-like quickness to the solemn-looking driver. Naturally the bus set off before he had time to sit down and he ended up stumbling over to the stairs, only just managing to grab the handrail before being flung to the floor. Steadying himself, he made his way awkwardly up to the top deck.

He walked through the city centre with more haste than usual, slaloming through the milling masses like a smartly dressed skier, and arrived at the office at 9.30am. It was less busy than normal, a plus because Rick really wanted to avoid talking to anyone but his boss.

The corridor at the top of the stairs was clear, save for an elderly cleaner dragging around a Henry Hoover. Rick set a course for the double doors to the main office but as he started moving, Dylan walked out of the store cupboard at the far end of the corridor carrying a bundle of fresh contracts under his arm. He strode towards the double doors, clearly about to address his underling.

Rick pretended he hadn't seen him and looked at his watch for longer than it took to read the dial. Dylan was about ten paces away from the doors and closing in, whereas Rick was only five paces away. Just then the cleaner walked between them, too engrossed in hoovering to notice Dylan was about to walk straight into her. Dylan stopped and cleared his throat impatiently.

'Sorry, love, I'll move it.' The cleaner slowly pulled the hose, sliding the hoover out of Dylan's path. That bought Rick the few seconds he needed to slip through the doors.

'Thank you, Henry,' Dylan said, ignoring the cleaner.

Rick saw McNabb through the large window that made up the top half of the inner wall of his office. He was talking to Greg, one of the team leaders. There were three chairs next to the door and only the first was occupied. Rick took the third, as if he were in a public toilet and the chairs were urinals.

The other occupant was a younger man whom

Rick had never seen before. He assumed he was waiting for an audience with Daniel McNabb.

'Alright?' Rick nodded at the lad and he nodded back.

Rick guessed he was about nineteen or twenty years old, probably looking for his first full-time job. He was wearing a new-looking Primark suit and his shoes had been polished the night before. In his hands was a thick black folder which he nervously pretended to be looking through. The first phase of interviewing had clearly been a success and the company were considering taking him on as a rep.

Greg exited the office and greeted the two of them pleasantly. The young man looked even more apprehensive, conscious that at any second he was about to enter the big boss's office. He and Rick both shifted round in their chairs to watch the door, knowing the man himself would soon step out like Richard Burton making an entrance at The Globe.

The door slowly opened revealing the holder of all the power at Gold Force, the man who had come from an Aberdeen council estate and taken over the world. Or at least set up the most profitable sales company in Greater Manchester.

McNabb was over six feet tall, around forty years of age, and his head was topped by short, greying hair that seemed to grip his head tightly. He was well built – he had some sort of military background of which Rick could never quite remember the details – and he had a light tan from a conference in some marvellously exotic part of the world.

'Hi, Rick,' he said. 'I must say, it's a pleasant surprise to see you here. Have you finally bowed down to the pressure and decided to come and brown nose me?' He chuckled.

'Maybe I'll have time to fit that in later. For now, I just need to have a quick word,' Rick replied.

'That's nay bother. I was going to invite you here before the meeting anyway – you must be a mind reader.' McNabb turned enthusiastically to the new man. 'Jamie, glad you could make it back for phase two. Come in.' He held the door back for Jamie to enter his office and then followed him in.

This is starting to look better, Rick thought; he wanted to talk to me first. For once he felt grateful for having Dylan as a team leader. He must have told McNabb about the previous day's failures. Rick was starting to see a way out that didn't involve him having to be too upfront about his opinions of the company.

Jamie left the office a few minutes later, grinning and generally looking a lot more relaxed.

'I'll see you at the meeting, then,' McNabb called to him as Jamie headed towards a whiteboard with a semi-circle of reps standing around it, keenly awaiting the next words of wisdom to be scribbled before them.

Rick got up and moved over towards McNabb's office.

'Okay, Rick, come in and take a seat.' Again, McNabb held the door open to welcome his visitor into his domain.

Rick didn't know whether he should speak first or wait to be addressed. His brain was whirling with several ways to start. Luckily, he didn't have to break the ice.

'Well, Rick, I believe you've been having problems in the field,' McNabb said understandingly.

Rick paused for a moment, trying to gather his thoughts. It was rare that he went into McNabb's office and it was an impressive room. One wall was covered by a large bookcase full of titles on business strategy and motivation; another had various oil paintings and framed photos of McNabb meeting local MPs and businesspeople. The polished oak desk was accompanied by a comfy-looking leather chair rather like a throne. Most MD's offices would have swivel chairs and computer desks, yet McNabb's room wouldn't have looked out of place in the Cluedo mansion.

'Yes, I'm finding it hard to sell,' Rick finally replied. 'It's been like this for a few weeks.' More like a few months!

'I had noticed your sales have been declining. I also notice that you don't look all that happy in the office.'

That was a shocker for Rick, even though it was true. He had been proud of how well he had hidden his discontent. Nobody ever noticed. But Daniel McNabb was very good at working out what people thought; it was how he'd got so far.

Rick chose his words carefully. 'If I'm honest, I haven't really been enjoying it. I seem to have lost my motivation for the work.'

'I understand how you feel, Rick. The truth is that some people just can't sell as well as others. I know that doesn't sound like an amazing revelation, but it's easily forgotten in this line of work. Every day we teach people that *anyone* can sell with the right attitude and a good work ethic. You have a great work ethic – I don't doubt that you want to work hard.' McNabb had a broad smile on his face that made Rick feel a little uneasy, even though he nodded his understanding.

'It puts us in a difficult position. I don't want to terminate you,' McNabb said earnestly.

I wish you would terminate me, Rick thought.

'I want to help you succeed and I have an idea. It's not a good time to lose your job. Next week we're sending a team on a road trip. I want you to go to Edinburgh with Dylan, Christine and someone else whom I've yet to pick. You're going to stay at the house of a friend of mine, and you'll spend each day out selling. There's no need to actually go to the Edinburgh office, so you'll be straight out into the field first thing, giving you more time on the doors. I think you can sell. Put the effort in and it will pay off. People come back from road trips having made much more cash than they would here. I trust you to work hard and hit big targets. What do you think?'

McNabb sat back in his chair but shifted slightly to one side, as if giving Rick space to consider his answer.

It wasn't exactly what Rick was looking for. He'd expected to be out of there by now, had even planned which big-brand coffee shop he was going to celebrate in. He didn't know how to react. *Come on, just say no, I'm leaving*, he thought.

'I think the trip sounds like a good idea. It might help me a lot,' he said out loud.

Brilliant, I have absolutely no balls.

All the confidence he had built up sitting outside McNabb's office had drained out of him like water through a colander.

'Excellent. Dylan will give you all the details later on. Anyway, I must get on before the meeting starts. Go out there today and put your best foot forward.'

Rick got up to leave.

'Oh, and make sure the rest of your body follows, of course,' McNabb chuckled as Rick walked out.

Feeling dejected, Rick walked back into the main office where the usual pitch practice and shit shooting was going on. The only option was to get on with things. He saw Christine by the water cooler and snaked his way through the crowded room to get to the most valuable point of any workplace.

'Hi, Rick, I thought you weren't coming in today for a second.' As usual she looked so full of beans she could stock a Little Chef.

'No, I came in early to see Daniel.' He expected this would get a laugh.

'I knew it! I knew you fancied him!'

'I bet you're just jealous,' Rick retorted in true cheeky-child style.

'You wish. Anyway, have you seen Sally? She hasn't been in this week?' Christine continued.

'No, don't think so – why?' In all honesty, he couldn't even remember who Sally was.

'Well, she hasn't been in since Thursday and I asked around and no one's seen her or knows where she is.' She shrugged her shoulders, expecting a reaction.

'This office is getting more and more Orwellian every week. People just disappear and it seems like they never existed.' Leaning in a little closer, Rick whispered conspiratorially, 'Bit spooky, don't you think?'

'Is everybody ready for the meeting?' someone shouted over the din, completely ruining Rick's conversation with Christine. These meetings were starting to fall at the most inconvenient times.

McNabb walked into the middle of the room and

the noise of affirmative cheering that followed quietened down to silence. He looked around to see how many were present. 'Good morning, everyone. Glad to see so many of you actually wanted to show up to work today.'

Many of those standing around burst into hysterical laughter. McNabb didn't seem too bothered by the blatant sycophancy.

'Firstly, I would like to introduce a new sales rep to the company. Everyone, give Jamie a big hand,' he said, pointing both arms straight at Jamie, like a compere introducing a comedian to the stage.

Jamie looked sheepishly around the room as everyone clapped.

'You're in for a real treat today, Jamie. You're about to discover how to become rich,' McNabb added, at which the room exploded into cheering again.

'Everyone in here has the potential to achieve whatever they want in life. Knocking on doors may not seem like the best life, but the saleswoman who trained me started off on the doors and she now owns an executive box at Old Trafford. You all remember Tessa Jansen from the awards ceremony?' He looked around at the nodding heads.

As McNabb went on with the meeting, Rick started to think back to the discussion they'd just had. He'd been told that some people just can't sell, but now he was being sent on a road trip with even longer hours out selling and was being subjected to a speech about how you could become a millionaire by selling. As much as Rick liked McNabb, he was beginning to understand him less and less.

○━● ●━○

Onto the bus and into the field again. Jamie had joined Dylan's team and would be spending the day going door to door with him. Afterwards he would have his final interview with McNabb and quite probably be offered the job. Rick didn't envy him.

'How are you feeling about this, mate?' Dylan asked him.

'I think it could be great. My family were a bit disappointed that I chose to work rather than go to university, but I could become rich,' Jamie replied hopefully.

'Yeah, too right. This will probably be the best decision you ever make. You don't need uni – £9,000 debt and no job is all you get from that. Though I'm sure Rick will disagree.' Dylan turned to look at Rick, waiting for a response.

'I loved uni. I met a lot of great people, got some life experience and even had a bit of fun,' Rick said, realising that he really needed to get in touch with the people he'd gone to university with. He hated Dylan's attitude. There were a lot of subjects they didn't agree on, and it wasn't a surprise to hear Dylan refer to the 'University of No Life'.

'You don't need a degree to do this job. Jamie, how old are you?' Dylan turned back to his new team member.

'Nearly nineteen,' Jamie answered.

'By the time you're Rick's age, you could be on a six-figure wage all because you got this job straight away.' Dylan was twenty-seven and wasn't all that far off a six-figure wage of his own.

'That would be so cool. Everyone would be well-shocked. I could go tell all the lads from school to piss right off.' Jamie looked very excited at the prospect.

'I know what you mean, mate. I love walking through the estate I used to live on and seeing the guys I used to go to school with. They still live in the same shitty council flats.' Dylan had told this story several times; he was enjoying meeting someone who didn't know it.

'Do you go on these council-house laughter tours very often, Dylan?' Christine chipped in. Rick had to smile at that.

'You two can smirk all you want. At the end of the day, I had a tough upbringing and had to survive it, just like Daniel. That's why we get on so well,' he said seriously.

'I hope it all goes well today,' Jamie said. He had the kind of optimism for the job that Rick had once

possessed, back when he started. He hoped Jamie
wouldn't cock it up.

o-• •-o

'So it's not exactly the result you were hoping for.'
Callum had listened to Rick's story very patiently.
He had wanted to interrupt on several occasions to
question his friend's sanity but in the end he opted
for the calmer dig.

They had only been in The Earl ten minutes when
the tirade started. Rick had been in a foul mood all
day. The hours had dragged painfully, and he had
spent most of the afternoon constantly checking
his watch, convinced that time had slowed down.
Naturally, he had made no sales.

'It was the last thing I expected and wanted, so
typically it was the only result I could have ended
up with. Now I have to do the same shite job but
in sub-zero temperatures,' he complained bitterly.

There had been a briefing on the Edinburgh
job from Dylan after work. The team had been so
excited when he had showed them the maps of
the areas in which they would be working. There
were vast stretches of housing with so many
opportunities to strike gold that they felt like
Californian prospectors.

Rick had tried to appear happy about it. He'd even
thrown in a few bog-standard phrases common to

Gold Force, such as, 'We're going to clean up here.'

Christine had started perfecting her Scottish accent so she could get them killed whilst they were up there.

'Why is he sending you so far away?' Callum asked.

'There's this mate of his, Nathan Vaughn, who has a mini-mansion on the outskirts of Edinburgh. He and McNabb go way back; they both joined the company at the same time. While McNabb led his forces south, Vaughn stayed to take over the business world in Scotland.' That was about as much as Rick understood of the relationship.

'I can't believe you bottled quitting.' Callum sounded understandably frustrated.

'I know, I can't believe it either. What the hell do I do now?' Rick leaned back in his chair, awaiting Callum's response.

'I suppose you're just going to have to get on it with it. Go on the trip.' Callum allowed his gaze to drift to the bottom of his pint glass in a not-too-subtle hint.

'That's it? The sum total of all your wisdom? Just carry on?'

'I promise that if I think of a better solution, you'll be the first person I tell. Can we stop all this ranting now?'

'Yeah, sorry.'

'Or at the very least, save it until your midlife crisis. I'm looking forward to mine.'

Four

D ay one of the road trip began later than anyone had expected. Rick arrived at the large car park behind the office at 2pm to see Jamie waiting there. He hadn't known who the final member of the group was going to be and was surprised it was someone so new.

'Where do you think Dylan is? He said we were leaving at two.' Jamie had a rare ability to sound nervous even when asking the most mundane question.

'I don't know. He doesn't mind keeping us waiting,' Rick replied. Although Dylan claimed to hate tardiness.

The roar of an engine aborted the imminent awkward silence between the two reps, and they turned to see a newly valeted silver Mondeo pull into the car park. Dylan and Christine climbed out. Rick wondered how embarrassing Dylan's first sentence was going to sound. It was not quite as bad as he'd expected. 'Alright, guys, ready for a ride in Maximus?'

'Are you sure Maximus is going to get us there alright, Dylan?' Rick asked him, looking over his shiny transport for the week.

'Are you taking the piss? Of course it will. I only bought it last month. Insurance would be a killer to most people, but I've got it sorted.'

Rick shouldn't have been surprised that Dylan believed the speed limit was only advisory. As they flew up the M6 at 85 mph, he watched the other cars turn into colourful streaks. Christine was sitting in the passenger seat, her head stuck out of the window like an excitable dog. 'I love speeding,' she shouted over the noise of the wind. 'You should try putting your head out of the window, Dylan. Makes the journey more fun.'

'What?' Dylan called back.

She settled back into her seat and repeated her pitch.

'Only if you want the emergency services to scrape you off the motorway,' Dylan replied.

'If it's the only way I'll meet a man in a sexy uniform this week, then I insist you crash right now!'

'You said this week. How often do you normally try to pull uniformed men?' Rick spoke for the first time in half an hour.

'All the time! Only last week I pretended to faint at a fun run to see who would help me. It backfired when an old man from St John's Ambulance attempted CPR on me,' she said laughing.

The car suddenly slowed down. On the hard

shoulder ahead was a police car that Dylan had only just noticed in time. *Maybe we'll all be experiencing those sexy uniformed men soon*, Rick thought.

'Shit, sorry about that. Coppers will try to catch anyone out. It doesn't matter to them how important our business is, they still set these traps,' Dylan snorted.

'How are they setting traps? You're the one speeding. It's hardly fair to accuse them of being Dick Dastardly!' Rick's voice exploded with more venom than he'd intended.

'Alright, calm down. I'm just joking. You want us to get there quickly, don't you? No need to get in a mood with me.' Dylan looked both surprised and amused by Rick's tone.

After an incredibly long service-station break, where Dylan insisted on having three coffees, the team got back on the road and carried on. It wasn't until daylight started to fade that they saw a large white cross over a blue sign welcoming them across the Scottish border. Cheers rang out, after which they all tried welcoming each other in Gaelic.

o—• •—o

They reached Edinburgh after nightfall, by which point they were too tired to celebrate their arrival. By the light of the well-spaced street lamps, they could see large gardens fronting sturdy town houses and sandstone Victorian tenements. They were obviously in the land of the professional classes.

Dylan pulled into the drive of Vaughn's massive, detached house. The lawn was mowed into lines like a football pitch. At the far end was a table with six chairs and a closed parasol shoved awkwardly through the centre. Judging by how wet the table was, it looked like the garden furniture had been neglected.

The four reps stretched their limbs gratefully as they climbed out of the car. Dylan marched up to the large front door, swinging the key he'd been given on his left index finger. 'Here it is, home from home.' He opened the door and they hurried inside.

The house had five large bedrooms, two of them with en-suite bathrooms. Dylan and Christine took those, whilst Jamie and Rick settled into the two smaller ones. By then Rick just wanted to go straight to bed and forget the predicament he was in. After a quick sink wash, he stripped to his boxers, hit the hay and sank into the comfortable bed.

Five

Early on Monday morning, the large kitchen was as abuzz as a room with four people in it could be. It didn't surprise anyone that Christine was just as energetic at 7.30am as she was the rest of the time. She had a fresh exuberant look and a face that lacked the bags and sags that dominated Rick's. Dylan was already dressed in his smart black suit and looked ready for a day selling. Jamie obviously hadn't slept well and yawned his way through questioning Dylan about technique. 'So, how *do* I get them to like me?'

Rick realised he'd left the bag he normally took into the field with him in the hallway and went to fetch it. He put it on the kitchen top and took out the paperwork, checking he had the correct literature for the day. Realising that a well-ordered bag wasn't going to help, he gave up after about thirty seconds and decided to make a cup of coffee instead.

After breakfast, Dylan decided it was time to inform the team about their mission. 'It's briefing time, everyone,' he said, standing up importantly in front of his three team members.

Rick carried on sipping his second cup of coffee, knowing he was going to gain nothing.

'This is the big one. It's D-Day. The beaches are out there and it's going to be tough, but we will make a lot of cash today.'

Whilst Dylan carried on talking, Rick's eye glanced along the kitchen top he was leaning on. He picked up a discarded A4 leaflet folded into three with a picture of a large glass building on the front. It was a scene shot at night; every window was lit up and several people were entering and leaving through the large lobby. The orange text on the front read *THE LIGHT*.

Opening the leaflet, Rick was disappointed to see it was merely a conference centre and the inner pages showed an auditorium with row after row of fold-up seats facing a large stage.

'Is that more interesting than what I'm saying, Rick?' Dylan piped up.

It obviously was, but Rick responded in the correct fashion. 'Sorry, mate. You were saying?'

As Dylan carried on with what he was saying, Rick shoved his papers into his bag, leaflet and all.

○—● ●—○

If that was D-Day, Rick thought, then I'm stuck in the south of England whilst Dylan and Christine storm Sword Beach. Ten hours of being told to piss off made him realise he wouldn't be going home for tea and medals.

There wasn't much of interest on his patch. Even the missing-dog poster stuck to a telegraph pole was faded; the water had leaked under the Sellotape and turned the paper an odd shade of purple. Rick wondered whether Mr Choo Choo would ever be found, or if he too was doomed to wander the streets of suburbia until the trumpets sounded and four very scary equestrians showed up.

For a moment Rick pictured the Dalmatian from the conference on its very own poster, caught mid-jive, its soulless black plastic eyes fixed on him.

After several hours of getting nowhere, Rick met the rest of the team and they stopped selling. They returned to the house after grabbing a quick bite from the chip shop. Christine had insisted on this, due to never having had a battered Mars bar before. Rick had ordered a cheeseburger and was surprised to find out that you had to order the bread bun separately. He was even more surprised that the chip shop's take on a cheeseburger involved sandwiching a slice of cheese between two burgers and battering them together. By that point he was so hungry that he didn't have any problem digesting the Heart-Attack Special.

Whilst they were reclining in the lounge, Dylan started to regale the group with a story.

'He was right up in my face, a great big bearded bastard with breath that could strip wallpaper. He said that if I didn't get off his property, he'd get his cricket bat and bash my face in.' He paused, trying to look suave before continuing. 'So I asked him if he was looking forward to the Ashes. It turned out the bat wasn't just a weapon and he was a fan. I soon had his signature on the contract,' he finished proudly.

'I think you were quite lucky then, Dylan,' Christine said.

'Luck didn't come into it. How did you get on, Jamie?' Dylan had tired of describing his own adventures and moved on to quizzing an underling.

'I don't think it went well, mate.' Jamie sounded genuinely disappointed.

'Wrong attitude, Jamie. You have to be more positive,' Dylan snapped. Turning to Rick, he demanded, 'Did you lose your attitude?'

Rick returned his gaze, then looked at Jamie and then Christine. They were all looking back at him expectantly. It was one of those moments that Rick dreaded, where all he wanted to do was admit the truth but couldn't. Dylan was already completely indoctrinated into the sales mindset and Christine was far too positive to see the bad in anything. There was only Jamie whom his words would affect.

'Yes, I think I did for a bit. You see, Jamie, what Dylan keeps saying is true. You need a positive attitude no matter how hopeless things might look.' He decided to play the game, having seen enough people listen to Dylan's teaching to realise that it often did work. He wasn't sure whether Jamie would take to the shrewder elements, but hoped he would at least get something from the job.

Shortly afterwards, Rick skulked upstairs to his room to avoid the others for a while. He sat on the bed and contemplated his position yet again. The day had gone just as badly as it would have done back home. Normally he would have thought nothing of it, but this time he had McNabb's words to consider. Rick knew McNabb had faith in him and he was letting him down. And even if he didn't care about the work, he had to think seriously about money. He was nearly broke and really needed to sell.

Later, when he ventured back downstairs, Dylan cornered him in the hall. 'Rick, a word please,' he said, opening the door to an unused dining room.

Rick walked straight in, followed by Dylan who quietly shut the door behind them. 'Take a seat.'

In the centre of the room stood a bare table surrounded by six chairs. There were no placemats. It didn't look like Vaughn was the type for dinner parties.

'Why did you say it was hopeless out there?' Dylan seemed calm as he asked this.

'I didn't. I just said...'

'You implied it was!' Dylan's voice rose only slightly. 'Don't think I don't notice the sarcasm that underpins everything you say to the team. Don't try to undermine me, Rick.'

'I don't know what you're on about,' Rick said with genuine surprise.

'The reason you haven't sold much is that your attitude stinks. Is it any wonder customers don't want to talk to you?'

Rick went quiet, not sure how to respond.

'Well, Rick, do you have anything to say?'

'I know I'm not doing well. That's why I was sent up here, to improve.'

'Make sure that you do. And keep your smart-arse comments to yourself. You look stupid when you say them and you make me look stupid, too. Do you want to make me look stupid?' Dylan, still not understanding how rhetorical questions worked, paused in expectation of an answer.

'No, I don't,' Rick answered.

'Well, thanks for that, mate.' Dylan obviously didn't think that sarcasm was beneath him.

'I promise I'll do better tomorrow,' Rick sighed.

'Thanks, I appreciate that.' Like the flick of a switch, Dylan was back to his normal annoying self. 'Let's get a drink.'

They entered the lounge to see that Christine had cracked open a bottle of vodka and was mixing it with whatever fizzy drinks she could find. Rick silently accepted a glass. He was still in mild shock at Dylan's words. He would have admitted a thousand times that he could be sarcastic, and his comments did sometimes spill over into the pool of insubordination, but his words never held any real animosity.

'Right, let's play some drinking games,' Dylan suggested.

Oh great, Rick thought. *Forced fun!*

'I know a great one – Run Piggy Run,' Christine piped up giddily.

'No, there's only one we can play – it's a Gold Force classic,' Dylan claimed. 'It was created by non-other than Tony Barr!' He waited for an astonished reaction.

'Who was he again?' Christine asked, diluting her Coke with more vodka.

'He used to work in our office. The man was an absolute legend.'

'I remember him,' Rick said. 'I remember him being led out of the office by the Fraud Squad.'

'That had nothing to do with Gold Force!' Dylan snapped. 'He was a great rep and he created the company drinking game.' He made it sound as if having a company drinking game were quite normal.

Dylan's 'hilarious' game was one he was good at, so he barely had to drink a shot. 'You're holding your glass in the right hand. Down it... You have to say it without vowels – two fingers!'

'This doesn't make any sense.'

'Not understanding the rules, four shots.'

As the vodka and fizzy Vimto flowed, Rick noticed that Jamie was avoiding eye contact with the group. The more he did it, the more Dylan leaned over and slapped his back or ruffled his hair, as though Jamie were an urchin who'd just been given sixpence. Even Christine started to feel uncomfortable.

Eventually the game ended. Dylan howled with laughter as Jamie silently got to his feet and left, stumbling over a footrest as he went.

o—● ●—o

After a long soak in the bath, Rick was crossing the landing when he heard a pleading whine coming from the small room next to his. He stopped to listen.

'Just let me give it a try, Dad.' Jamie had left the door ajar. Rick edged slightly closer, his bare feet muffled by the thick carpet.

'I know, I know. But I can do this. The road trip's my big chance.' Jamie's words were coming out disjointedly as he tried to sound more sober than he actually was. It was a trick that wasn't fooling his father.

Rick felt a little guilty eavesdropping and was about to walk away, but he couldn't resist it. He had to hear at least one voice that wasn't singing the praises of the company. Just hearing one person who wasn't obsessing over their job gave him a little comfort.

'It's too late for that now, Dad. I'm working for Gold Force and I'm going to do well. Dylan and Rick both said I can make it,' Jamie said with forced hopefulness.

Rick couldn't listen any more. He didn't like how the lad saw him as a potential role model when he really didn't believe in what they were doing. Jamie had clearly listened to his advice and believed he could be rich some day. Rick hated himself for potentially trapping the new recruit in the job.

Six

The gathering around the breakfast bar the next morning was a little quieter and more subdued than it had been the previous day. Rick assumed that Dylan was still annoyed with him after their rather heated discussion. Neither did Jamie look happy. Rick didn't blame him; it must be difficult to have parents that criticise your attempts to do well in the world. He felt lucky he barely saw his own parents. That way, at least they hadn't realised how unremarkable his life had become.

'It's another big day today, people.' Dylan had lost his usual pep-talk verve. Rick wondered if he already knew he was going to do well and had stopped caring how the rest of the team performed.

'I love Scottish people. What a great accent,' Christine said, sounding like her usual self.

'That's it, is it? Thousands of years of culture, famous authors, several inventions, and you just like the way they pronounce "sausages",' Rick said.

'I like the way they tell me to "pess off". It sounds funny.' She laughed childishly.

'Come on, let's get started,' Dylan ordered.

०-● ●-०

He'd only knocked on thirty doors and Rick already felt like he needed a sit down. Energy had leaked out of him like sewage from the pipes of a badly-plumbed house. All the reactions were the same; nobody was interested.

He seemed to have drawn the shortest of a bunch of very short straws. As the bus arrived, the whole team took a collective gulp as they saw the area they had been assigned. To say it was run down would be an understatement. There was nothing at all welcoming about the place, and the drab grey blocks of flats loomed over them like ugly bouncers about to kick their heads in. Children on bikes circled the balconies, pointing at the team like they were enemy invaders and an ambush was due. The local community centre looked as though the community hadn't met there since Logie Baird's new creation was first displayed. The boarded-up windows exploded with colour courtesy of the local graffiti artist who was certainly no Banksy.

They stopped outside an abandoned job centre. Dylan usually referred to them out loud as 'Yob Centres', although he didn't seem too keen to make that witticism whilst being observed by their new group of friends.

After a quick meeting, they split up nervously to go about their business despite Rick and Jamie insisting that they should stick together.

'You'll be fine, I promise,' were the only words

that Dylan could think of to reassure them.

As Rick set off to his collection of streets, he felt like he was in downtown Basra. It didn't just feel unsafe; some of the things he saw were just plain weird. Passing a small park, he thought he saw a man in a Victorian-style butterfly-catcher's outfit, complete with large net. On closer inspection, the man was actually holding a stick with a carrier bag of dog turds attached to the end of it.

Rick decided to risk doing his job. Nobody answered at the first few flats he approached, for which he was grateful. He came to one open door where a strong smell of weed and dog faeces was drifting out and quickly moved on. It soon became clear that the type of person who lived in this area didn't care how they paid for their energy. Many of them probably didn't bother paying at all.

In the past when Rick had been unhappy with work, he would sabotage his efforts. He would put people off by making the change to N-ergise sound incredibly complicated and not worth it. He knew the customers wouldn't save much, so he didn't feel guilty about it. No, it was a liberating feeling; he was bringing the empire down from within. He was the Oskar Schindler of the energy business; none of his shells were going to explode with pointless billing changes.

His mobile vibrated in his trouser pocket. Dylan was checking up on him.

'Hi, mate, how are you doing?' Rick asked.

'I'm doing incredibly well, as usual. The question is, how are you doing?'

'Not great. No sales.'

'Come on, Rick. I'm deadly serious – you need to pull your finger out,' Dylan said angrily.

'I'm trying, but I don't think selling in a different geographical location is really making any difference,' Rick hissed though clenched teeth, feeling like he was about to explode.

Dylan's tone was calmer when he replied. 'I thought I told you I don't like it when you're a smart-arse. But do I need to ask you what your bonus is going to be next month. And that's not the only problem.'

'What do you mean?'

'Do you really want to let Daniel down?'

The words smacked Rick right in the guts and for a second he was speechless. He felt a fresh jolt of anxious energy that he hadn't expected. He actually felt he needed to sell. 'I'll get back to it. I just need to calm down a bit.'

'Good. I'll see you later,' Dylan said and hung up.

o–• •–o

Dylan's ball-breaking started to have its desired effect. Rick ran around the estate like his life depended on it and he really tried hard at each door he knocked on, but they were slammed in his face. Inwardly he cursed each one of the residents.

After an hour he was exhausted. He stopped for a breather outside a block of flats eight floors high. There was no sign of any more cycling hyenas. It was too early in the day for any of the residents to be up, so the building stood tall and mute. The door to the lobby was barely attached to its hinges and many of the windows had been smashed from the outside. The strange thing was that it wasn't just the windows on the lower floors.

On the opposite side of the road was a row of shops with one floor of flats above them accessible by a staircase from the street. It had an added level of security in the form of a buzzer-operated door. On the ground floor were the usual off-licences and tanning shops. There was also a kebab shop that proudly displayed its three-star hygiene certificate. It being open before midday gave a Rick an idea of what kind of diet the locals had.

He crossed the street and looked through the window into the dimly-lit interior, trying to decide whether to get a can of Coke. On the grubby back wall there was a large map of the area with a circle in the centre identifying the location. There were larger circles outside that one, moving gradually away from the shop. Rick assumed that was to work out how much to charge people as the delivery man got further away, although he wished they were there to work out a nuclear fallout range. An atomic explosion would be a good renovation plan and would explain the brazenness of the cockroach Rick could see scurrying under the counter.

He managed to force his mind away from his apocalyptic fantasy and decided to try the door next to the takeaway. The drink could wait. He pressed the buzzer to Flat 1 and heard a timid female voice respond. 'Hello, can I help you?' she asked.

'I'm here about your gas and electric.' Rick made it sound more official than sales-like. Technically he was misleading her, but it was nothing thousands before him hadn't done. The buzzer sounded and he let himself in. The door at the top of the stairs opened and a woman in her mid-forties looked down nervously at him.

He took the stairs two at a time. 'Hi, my name's Rick. I'm in the area to check that you're happy with your gas and electric supplier,' he said, trying to appear positive.

'Yes, I suppose I am.' She sounded confused and her voice shook slightly.

'Great, but you could save up to £200 a year on your bills with N-ergise. A lot of your neighbours have found it's easy to change over and start saving straight away.' He pulled a contract out of his bag. 'What I can do for you is work out exactly how much you'd save. Do you have somewhere I can lean?'

As he stepped forward and pointed to a small desk in the hall, the woman flinched back out of the way. 'Er, yes I suppose so.' A hand went up to her face and wiped away a trace of a tear.

'Thanks.' He was already inside. 'How much do you normally pay for your bills?' He began writing the address on the contract.

'Fifty pounds a month,' she replied.

'Is that for just gas or both?' Rick asked in surprise.

'That's for all my bills. I've only been here for two months and that's what it cost so far.' Another tear was running down her face.

'Really? That's incredibly cheap! I wish I could get mine that low.' He tried his best fake laugh.

'This flat is owned by the charity. They subsidise the bills.'

Rick stopped writing and straightened up, turning uneasily to face the woman. He stopped thinking about the contract and his mind returned to normal. The worn-out look, the red puffed-up eyes, the tears streaking down her cheeks, he had ignored them all. 'What charity is that?' he said slowly.

'It's one that looks after abused women,' she said simply.

'Oh God, I'm sorry. I'd better be leaving now.' Shoving the contract back in his bag, he hurried through the door, embarrassed and desperate to escape.

'That's alright, love. You weren't to know,' she said as he retreated. She closed the door slowly behind him.

He breathed a sigh of relief as he burst onto the street. How had it come to this? How had he become so desperate to sell that he barged into an abused woman's home? She'd said she had only been there for a couple of months; for all Rick knew, the escape from her violent partner could have been all too recent.

His anger was rising and he had a sudden urge to do something destructive. He felt his mobile buzzing again in his pocket. Maybe it was someone who could calm him down, make him feel better.

It was Dylan. 'How's it going, Rick?' He didn't sound very cheerful.

'To be perfectly honest with you, it hasn't been my best day. And, as you know, I've had some stinkers in this job.' Rick thought he was managing his anger surprisingly well.

'Will you calm down? Hey, I can see you.' Dylan hung up, leaving Rick to spin around in an attempt to spot him. At first he just saw another gang of dangerous-looking youngsters leaning over the railings on a flight of stairs to the flats, but when he turned back round, Dylan had materialised.

'What's going on,' he barked at Rick.

'It's going to shit, is what's going on.'

'You're seriously losing your attitude. You *have* to

get it back,' Dylan said patronisingly.

'That's not going to happen! I don't know if you've noticed, but my positive attitude fucked off some time last year and isn't planning a comeback,' Rick yelled.

The gang of lads on the stairs heard him and started laughing raucously. Two of them got up and lumbered over to where confrontation was taking place.

'Where do you get off talking to me like that? I'm your team leader! I'm trying to help you and you talk to me like I'm a twat.' Dylan sounded as pissed off as Rick did.

'I'm not really in the mood to talk to you right now, Dylan.' Rick turned to leave. The camel's back had been well and truly broken; for him the war was over.

'Where the fuck do you think you're going? You don't walk away from me!' Dylan was about to follow but the two yobs approached him, the bigger of them standing between Dylan and the retreating Rick.

'Have you got a fag?' the smaller one spat.

'I don't smoke,' Dylan replied, his gaze travelling over the big lad's shoulder to Rick, who was speed-walking away.

'I ken you've got some, everyone does.' His claw-like hand went into the pocket of his tracksuit top. That was too much for Dylan, who turned around and sprinted away from the two boys. They both laughed as he fled between two large blocks of flats and out of view.

o—• •—o

Rick walked quickly to the end of the street and disappeared down a snicket. What had happened didn't quite register straight away. *Have I just shouted at my boss and told him that I hate my job? Have I actually spoken my mind for the first time in my life? I should have tried this years ago.*

He suddenly felt very liberated. He knew that most people wouldn't consider his actions to have been particularly brave, but for him they were. He had never been confrontational and always shied away from fights, so he'd always assumed that he wasn't brave, but now he was Richard the Lionheart.

I'll do a runner from work! They couldn't possibly find me. All it would take would be a bus ride back into town and the world would be my oyster. A great escape was just what the slightly irresponsible doctor ordered. The ultimate dream could be lived out.

Hurrying back to the bus stop, Rick's mind buzzed with exciting thoughts on how to spend the rest of his afternoon. An idea sprang up: head further north, right up to the Highlands. He fantasised about getting lost in the wilds like William Wallace.

As he got on the bus, Rick realised that he must have been smirking because the driver gave him a funny look when he took his ticket.

On the edge of the estate, Rick saw Jamie standing on the pavement outside a decrepit block of flats. His first instinct was to duck down; he didn't want any of the team to know where he was going.

The driver was looking in his mirror at him, totally perplexed. When Rick straightened up in his seat, he started laughing and continued with his laughing fit for a good ten minutes. Other passengers turned towards the window, trying to avoid making eye contact with the nutter.

As they neared the city centre, Rick felt a surge of excitement. For the first time on his trip to Edinburgh, he was actually going to see the place. It wasn't long before the menacing brutalist buildings gave way to tall, elegant, Victorian terraces and Rick spied minarets, spires and chimneys across the cityscape.

Before disembarking, the most striking of images caught his eye: the castle, perched sturdily atop an enormous rock. Rick gazed at its towers, turrets and flagpoles and hoped he'd get the chance to visit it.

The city was bustling as tourists of every nation milled about happily. Now that Rick was no longer at work, he felt like one of them. What was the most touristy thing he could do?

Rick pondered this whilst he passed the shops and bars. *What about paying a human statue to dance? What happens if you rob one? Are they allowed to chase after you, even if no money has been dropped in the bucket*? He could find out. He felt he could do anything, like go to the castle or to the pub or a museum. This business trip could turn into the ultimate pleasure trip.

Rick hadn't been on holiday for three years because he either couldn't afford it or had nobody to go with. The last one had been Ibiza; he'd thought it overrated and the people there were horrible. They were the type of idiots you saw on a night out, but they acted like that throughout the day as well. A location scout for the Al-Qaeda propaganda machine would choose Ibiza if they wanted to make a really condemnatory piece about western decadence.

But he was on holiday in Edinburgh and all good holidays began with a drink, so Rick found the nearest pub. It didn't bother him that he would be drinking alone; the important thing was that he was in the pub when he should have been working. He was beating the system.

His selected drinking hole was in a cellar. The jukebox was loudly blaring out some non-Gaelic music as he strolled into the half-full bar and waited patiently to be served.

'What can I get you, pal?'

'Pint of the light-brown stuff, please.'

As he sat and drank his expensive pint, Rick felt relaxed for the first time since his arrival in Scotland. He thought again about how to spend the rest of the day. The plan to travel further north and get lost in the wild didn't seem too outlandish. It would be quite easy, really: just one train journey and he would be away. *But do I really want to leave Edinburgh already,* he mused? He had only just got into the centre and knew he wouldn't get this chance again soon.

After finishing his pint, he wandered into the street. It was still very busy, although the sound of people talking was now being drowned out by a passing bagpiper. Maybe he did need an escape from the city.

Rick made up his mind and set off for the train station.

It looked like an inviting gateway to the unknown as Rick entered through the stone archway. Despite only having one pint inside him, he was feeling lightheaded. Where to go was the main question.

He sat on one of the metal benches opposite the departures board, scanned the screens and tried to identify the Scottish stations. Several familiar names appeared: Glasgow, Dundee, Stirling, Perth, Aberdeen, but they were no good. He needed to escape to somewhere smaller and more obscure.

He pondered the destination dilemma whilst

observing the hundreds of commuters and tourists. Idly, he slid his hand into his bag to find a cake bar and felt the edge of a piece of folded paper. Confused for a second, Rick pulled it out then remembered he'd shoved the leaflet for The Light in there with his stapled booklets.

On the back page was a map of the bottom half of Scotland showing the main routes to the conference centre. The first town to catch Rick's eye was Lochglen, which sounded like a splendid place. The map didn't give any indication of scale or how far apart the towns were, but that was a small detail that really didn't matter. He looked up at the boards and saw Lochglen was there.

As he approached the ticket desk, a question came to mind: single or return? He didn't know just how committed he was to this caper.

'One single to Lochglen please,' he said to the uninterested young man behind the glass.

Platform three was busy, so Rick had to resort to his people-dodging technique to jump on the train. As it pulled away, he looked back at the city he was leaving. He had escaped it all: the house, the customers, Dylan. They were all behind him now. Ahead lay the unknown, and Rick knew it would be better than what he'd just left.

o—● ●—o

During the journey his spirits ebbed slightly in a way that can only be caused by travelling a long distance by train. He was still excited, though, and spent most of the time looking out at the mountain peaks that rose up like bumps in the green-and-brown carpet of moorland.

He looked at his ticket. He had never heard of the town before and it felt like more of an adventure to pick somewhere strange. He had literally no idea what awaited him there.

Seven

Uncharacteristically, Dylan was pacing back and forth outside a rundown off-licence. The booze inside was exactly what he felt he needed, though he managed not to give in to his urge to buy several cans of cider. It wasn't the eighties and drinking on the job was unheard of, even in the Mercury Group.

He also wanted to keep his head as straight as an Assyrian archer's arrow. He was still slightly shaken from what happened with the two yobs, but he was damned if he was going to miss an opportunity to sell because of them.

'He's only a few minutes late,' Christine reassured him.

'He's fifteen minutes late. Rick is never, ever late to RVs.' Dylan had long suspected that Rick arrived early to spend less time knocking on doors, although he could never prove it.

Jamie was looking anxious; like Dylan, he knew that a quarter of an hour waiting around was at least two potential sales. He'd had none so far.

'Try his phone again,' Dylan told Christine. If they couldn't make the RV, a rep normally phoned or texted the team leader.

Christine informed Dylan that Rick's phone was switched off. 'Right, sod it. Let's get back to work,' he said irritably.

Jamie looked relieved as he hurried away.

Christine strolled over to Dylan. 'You're doing fine. Just calm down a bit,' she said, putting her hand on his shoulder and rubbing it lightly.

'He'll probably call me soon,' was all Dylan could think to say.

Eight

Rick stretched his limbs luxuriously as he stood up to leave the train. His first instinct was to check the timetable for his return journey but he stopped himself in time; Steve McQueen wouldn't have tried to find out how to get back to Stalag Luft III. No, he decided, he was going to walk out of the station utterly clueless.

When he left Lochglen station, he was hit by the desolation of the surrounding area. The town was a lot smaller than he'd expected, really more of a village. He could see a collection of large cottages and detached houses, a small church and what looked like an old-fashioned school with *Boys and Girls* engraved in the lintels above two entrances.

It seemed like it would only take a few minutes to walk right through to the other side of the place. The countryside was hilly, with vast forests stretching up the small mountains on all sides.

Rick chose a random direction to walk and was soon out of the village. He wondered whether he should go back and get supplies. *Just how long am I staying out here for*? In the end he decided to grab a bottle of water and some snacks from a local shop.

Turning round, he walked back quickly. The village square seemed to be the centre of activity, although there wasn't much going on. Two elderly gentlemen sat on a park bench whilst several pigeons milled around expectantly in front of them. Other than that, there was only the odd person going in and out of the shop and local pub. The rest of the buildings were either private homes, guesthouses or small businesses. It was a village where commerce was created by tearooms and shops selling knick-knacks.

A little bell chimed as Rick opened the shop door. The shopkeeper didn't look up from his paper as his customer started browsing the drinks and sweets.

Rick placed a bottle of water and a couple of flapjacks on the counter. The shopkeeper barely glanced at him or the items as he scanned them. Rick didn't find this particularly annoying, but concluded that it wasn't true what they said about people being much friendlier the further north you went.

Back on track, and walking away from civilisation, Rick felt relaxed. He'd never been one of those people who went into the countryside and claimed that it had a peacefulness that made him forget his troubles, but this time he really did feel lighter inside. *I'm running away from my life and I love it.*

He strolled along the pavement. After a couple

of hundred metres it disappeared and Rick found himself walking on a narrow grassy area by the side of the A-road. The problem was that there were too many nettles and Rick couldn't for the life of him identify that vital piece of nature's first-aid kit: a dock leaf. He decided it was time to leave the beaten track; that would have the added benefit of him not getting run over.

He climbed over a small wall, unconcerned about the green moss stains that smeared his black trousers. He landed awkwardly on the other side, caught his balance and then he was off. He scrambled over rough terrain, occasionally getting his feet caught in fallen branches that were tethered to the ground by grass that had grown there for years. He didn't care.

He came to the woods and decided to march straight through, confident that there was no danger of disturbing a shitting bear.

Looking at the trees and fauna around him, Rick realised how little he knew about nature; he couldn't name a single plant or shrub. If his granddad had been around, he'd have known what was what – he could identify birds from their calls and knew which side of a tree moss grew on.

Rick vividly remembered when they'd been rambling in the Peak District and Granddad had broken a branch off a tree and whittled a spear out of it with a penknife. Rick had been impressed, though in later years he began to doubt the old man's claim that a Zulu warrior had taught him how to do it.

Rick supposed it was a generational difference. His granddad and his friends had spent their summer holidays going into the woods for 'Famous Five' type adventures. Rick recalled his holidays being spent at his mate Philip's, playing on the N64, but he was happy reminiscing about his granddad and only realised then how much he missed him.

Rick came across a narrow, well-trodden path and decided to stick with it for a while. Even though it seemed like the less adventurous option, it was a pleasant route and it took him to the far side of the wood. There was a fast-flowing stream on the opposite side of a barbed-wire fence that separated the wood from a farmer's field.

It had taken an hour to get there after leaving the road, and Rick was satisfied he had covered a lot of ground. The pathway turned sharply and took him back towards the centre of the wood. Rick followed it until he spotted a large boulder that made an ideal seat.

Sitting down, he took a flapjack out of his bag and slowly began to eat it. The silence was reassuring and he felt comfortable, despite not being correctly dressed for the occasion. Then, in the distance, he heard a noise that dragged him from his calm sanctuary. It was the noise of a cheerful harmony that immediately grated on his nerves.

*'Keep the countryside tidy, keep the countryside clean
So the air can be fresh and the grass can be green.
So don't dump your rubbish, you know what we
mean...
Keep the countryside tidy, keep the countryside
clean.'*

The chorus was followed by the loud guffawing of half-a-dozen elderly voices. Rick heard their walking boots squelching on the damp grass, then he saw flashes of fluorescent green and yellows, and stupid sticks that looked like ski poles. They were ramblers – grey-haired and colourfully dressed ramblers. They had broken the beautiful silence with their singing and they were about to walk past.

They came along the path at a jaunty pace, smiling at Rick as they approached. A couple of them were holding black bin bags and long, thin metal sticks with plastic grabbers on the end. 'Afternoon,' they said pleasantly.

'Hello,' Rick responded.

'I hope you're not planning on dropping that wrapper, laddie,' said one man, who Rick guessed was the organiser. He pointed his stick like an angry Poseidon about to summon a storm.

'Oh, leave him alone, Derek. Don't mind him.

We're part of Scotland's battle against litter bugs. Derek's a little over-zealous,' said a woman Rick presumed was his wife. They were wearing matching boots with their trousers tucked into matching socks.

As the last of their group passed by, Rick noticed that they were wearing badges with a picture of a fizzy-drink can crossed out. Were they policing the woods? Derek certainly seemed like he was. Anyway, the peace had been destroyed and Rick decided to carry on walking in the opposite direction to Derek and his litter cops.

The woods had lost some of their appeal; they weren't as secluded as he had thought, and he knew he wasn't too far away from the main road. After more trudging, he found himself yet again at the edge of the tree line. Another field stretched out before him. *Sod it; I'm going straight through it.* He had no idea who owned the field – probably a farmer, though there were no animals to be seen. It was just a field of short grass.

After walking about fifty metres, Rick started to worry what would happen if the farmer was lurking around. They were some of the few people in Britain who were often armed. Would a farmer fire a warning shot first, or just go for the kill?

Worrying brought Rick back to his old state of mind. It was a common enough feeling for him, but he was determined not to let it bother him whilst he was crossing the phantom trigger-happy farmer's land. He knew it was naïve to believe that spending one afternoon doing something a bit crazy would change his outlook on life. He was still the same person, but now he felt like he was doing something daring.

The ground started to slope downhill; the field appeared to lead to a small road, beyond which was a town. Rick thought he should head in that direction and try to find somewhere to stay for the night. He was exhausted and his smart shoes were rubbing his feet into blisters.

As he left the field, Rick pondered again who might own it. Maybe it didn't have an owner and it was simply there, fulfilling no particular purpose. Was there still land like that in Britain? He had a notion that all land was owned, if not privately then by an organisation like the National Trust. He decided to look it up when he had time.

A strange sort of excitement hit him when he realised that so much time would become available now that his day job was ruined. He looked at his watch: it was 6.30pm. By now the team would have met up for a break and realised that Rick wasn't coming back for tea. He could picture it now: Dylan would be looking very annoyed because he'd have tried calling several times during the afternoon and he wasn't a man who liked to be ignored. Jamie would be confused as to how someone could run away from a job like this.

And then there was Christine. She was a different matter entirely, and Rick genuinely couldn't work out how she would feel or how she would react. He hoped she would be pleased, but he didn't know why. Rick had always wanted to be straight with Christine and tell her how much he disliked his job, but all he ever managed to do was joke about it. He was never sure if she realised how unhappy he really was.

Although he could picture how they would react at the RV, he didn't know what they would do. He guessed they'd go back to the house and Dylan would ring McNabb to tell him what had happened. McNabb's reaction was one that Rick couldn't even begin to speculate about.

Nine

It was dark by the time Rick reached the town he had spied from the field. The name of it was still a mystery because darkness had obscured any signs. He was too tired to carry on and, after spending half an hour wandering around the place, he found a reasonably priced B&B with vacancies. He decided to book one night there then go to a Chinese restaurant he'd noticed on the high street.

The restaurant wasn't very busy, yet it still felt weird being among people after his afternoon of complete solitude. Well, almost complete solitude. The tables around him were buzzing with travellers' talk which Rick found impossible to block out.

'Almost two hundred years it's been here, Nina.'

'Just four more areas left in this part of Scotland.'

'I think I prefer Canterbury on the whole.'

'I can't believe we've done it in every county!'

That last one made Rick turn around in astonishment. Two ladies in their fifties were sitting at the next table, one of them holding a dog-eared guide to potholing. He turned back to his chow mein and tried again to ignore the noise. Chairs were scraping, a child moaned, a man on a table opposite licked his knife. *That really is it, I can't stand these people!* Even so, he finished his meal. There was no point in storming out when he was hungry.

Thankfully the streets were quiet as Rick headed back to the B&B. He passed a pub called The Fleece. It sounded quite busy inside, but this was a rare occasion when Rick didn't feel like going in.

When he got back to his room, he lay on his bed and flicked on the TV. It was all rubbish: repeats of sitcoms he'd seen six times already, DIY shows, documentaries about the British coast and the usual reality TV.

He was getting irritable again. He'd thought that coming back to reality might relax him a bit and maybe even give him a much-needed boost of optimism. All it did was reinforce the feeling he'd had when he'd left the woman's flat earlier. It was all just bollocks.

Rick wondered what the woman was doing now. *At least it was me and not Dylan who called round,* he thought. He hated to think what Dylan's reaction would have been to her negative attitude. Maybe if Christine had been there, she would have known what to say. She would have made the woman feel better.

Ten

The depleted team sat in silence in the well-furnished front room of the borrowed mansion. The evening meal had been tense. Dylan was fairly quiet after he'd eventually calmed down.

He had ranted the entire bus journey home about Rick and his irresponsibility. 'I try so hard to help him. I train him, I offer him my wisdom, I take him under my wing and this is what he does. He goes AWOL on a road trip,' he fumed as Christine stared out of the window, watching the tall blocks of flats slip away.

None of them had sold much: Jamie had his usual score of zero; Christine two, and for the first time in years Dylan had only made just one sale.

The usual energy expected of an N-ergise sales team just wasn't there. Instead, there was silence. Jamie looked longingly at the widescreen TV taking up most of one corner of the front room. He daren't switch it on or even ask to.

Christine was slumped across two cushions on the black-leather sofa, trying to decide whether or not it would be appropriate to slip out for a walk. She had learned when she was young that she should always make the best of a bad situation – she'd been in one too many of those. But she knew this one would pass; in a few days she would be back in Manchester and able to see her family and her vast network of friends.

She'd spent much of the evening wondering where Rick was. She wasn't too worried. He could look after himself. But she really did want to know what he was doing and why he hadn't come back.

Lazily she took out her mobile and checked the time: 9.30pm. *Come on, Rick, come home. I don't want to be stuck here with just these two. I could do with hearing an amusing simile about the situation we're in.* He'd probably say something like, 'This house is like an upper-class Guantanamo Bay.' No, he'd come up with something better than that.

She glanced over at Dylan, who still looked annoyed. Christine wouldn't have been surprised if he was worried as well. She knew he hadn't phoned Daniel and probably wouldn't until morning. It wasn't Dylan's fault that Rick had left – there was nothing he could have done about it.

During his outburst on the bus, Dylan had finally explained to the rest of the team what had happened between him and Rick – although he omitted the bit about nearly being mugged by a child. Christine had noticed the tension building between Dylan and Rick; even before the road trip she'd seen the looks Rick shot at Dylan and the way he rolled his eyes at his comments. Rick used to take the mick in a light-hearted way, but she was starting to worry that now he actually disliked Dylan.

Christine had always liked Dylan. She didn't always appreciate the way he spoke to people, but knew that there was never any malice intended. He was just a bit odd, not quite on the same page as others. Then again, Gold Force seemed to attract that sort of person, so he didn't seem so strange at work.

She got up and stretched, her hands almost touching the ceiling. It was time for bed; she didn't want to stay up all night guessing where Rick was. He would call in the morning, she was sure of it.

Eleven

Remembering his mobile was still switched off, Rick fished it out of his pocket. It was tempting to bring the blank screen back to life and see what he'd been missing but he resisted the urge, knowing exactly what would happen. There would be several missed calls and messages asking where the hell he was. *Maybe Callum's texted me*, he thought. *He'll be interested to find out how I'm getting on.* Although Rick preferred to save the story for a face to face at the pub.

He fell asleep watching *Some Mother's Do 'Av 'Em*. It was early and he got a good night's rest before waking at 7.10am, it was the first time in years he had actually wanted to get up early.

The dining room was decorated in a vintage style – either that, or it had been decorated in 1979 and kept that way. Frank Spencer would have felt at home there. The wallpaper was dull beige with white stripes, and the framed pictures were mostly of the local area. According to the brass plaques, some of them dated as far back as 1928. The most recent was of a footballer from 1976; he was presumably from the local team and had signed the photo. He had long hair and very short shorts, in stark contrast to the 1931 team picture where it was all short-back-and-sides and three-quarter-length shorts.

The elderly owner of the B&B brought out a trolley with a large, cosy-covered pot of tea. Some minutes later, she placed a full English in front of Rick and a toast rack of mixed bread. He found it curious that there were so many breakfast implements still available, despite hardly anyone using them.

The breakfast was delicious: two rashers of bacon, two fried free-range eggs, two sausages, half a grilled tomato, a hash brown, mushrooms and baked beans. What more could you ask for? Some fried bread would have been nice, but Rick wasn't about to complain. He felt well-fed and unhurried as he read the paper.

He had made his mind up the previous night about what to do next. Boring TV and annoying people had convinced him that this escape wasn't enough. He was still too close to civilisation.

He left the B&B early and decided to stock up on supplies. There weren't many people around; the only living thing that showed Rick any attention was a cat with a Hitler moustache. Rick maintained eye contact with it for a few seconds before realising that he was only a few metres away from where he wanted to be.

The Tesco Express was nearly empty, save for a

local man buying the *Daily Sport*. Rick wondered what kind of supplies adventurers usually bought; he was pretty sure they didn't get them from Tesco's, but a lack of overpriced outdoor-pursuit shops meant that he had to make do.

He made a mental checklist:

Plasters

Tissues

A one-litre bottle of water

Nourishment in the form of chocolate

A sandwich

He found his supplies and took them to the counter. The cost made him wince slightly as he paid by card. He didn't dare to check how much was left in his account, but he figured he should get used to being poor. It felt weird to think of a man in twenty-first-century Britain living as a pauper. Obviously, there were people living below the poverty line, but Rick found it hard to contemplate that he would be joining them soon. *Me? From a safe middle-class background and soon unable to afford a comfy toilet roll?*

With the food and drink tucked away in his bag, Rick left the shop. As he set off on the path next to a B-road which snaked out of the town, he noticed that the Für-hrer was licking one more ball than his namesake possessed.

He felt very self-conscious at being the only pedestrian on the path. He wondered what the drivers thought of him as they drove past – it probably looked a bit odd to see a man in a suit with a satchel out on a country road. Yet again, he longed to be somewhere more private.

He passed a large field, similar to the one he had crossed the previous day. Was it a good idea to leave the road? He didn't know where he was going so it didn't really matter how lost he got. Having not been shot by a farmer last time he'd trespassed, he wasn't worried.

He repeated his road-avoidance technique and was soon strolling merrily through the field. It was an uphill gradient so he couldn't see very far ahead, but that wasn't off-putting. He was heading into the unknown and had all day to do it.

The slight incline made Rick's legs ache. During the previous year he'd become more prone to occasional aches. If he ever found himself on the floor, which would be a ludicrous situation in itself, he found himself making a pained, yet restrained, noise as he got up.

His attempts to ease the pain of his blisters with plasters wasn't working very well. After each step, he felt them rubbing. He started to wonder what the point of all this was. Had he really achieved something so great by bunking off? The team would all be going back to the mansion that evening. They'd have baths, raid the fridge and recline on a massive leather sofa. Meanwhile Rick would still be wandering around outdoors like a very pathetic Grizzly Adams.

He wasn't sure what he was going to say when he met them again. He'd have to go back eventually, and he'd been putting off thinking about the reunion. As he'd left the pub in Edinburgh, an ugly thought had poked its head around the door in his mind: what would Dylan say about it, and what would McNabb do about it. But Rick had slammed the door shut and started his journey. Now he was flapping a bit. He couldn't imagine the look on McNabb's face; he'd seen him angry a few times, but it was rarely directed at an individual. Would he be more confused than annoyed? It certainly wasn't what people usually got sacked for, although the sacking would definitely happen.

He stopped walking for a moment. Sighing, Rick realised he knew exactly how McNabb would react: he would be disappointed. It was odd how letting people down could make someone feel worse than enraging them. McNabb genuinely wanted Rick to make it in his world, he'd tried to help him, and all Rick had done was run away when the best opportunity to succeed was presented to him.

He sat on the damp grass, pulled his knees up, rested his forehead on them and tried to fathom out why he'd been so stupid. *I could have got out earlier. I should have quit months ago.*

Rick thought about the good references he would

have got. He'd blown any chance of leaving work with any dignity; everyone in the office would know what he had done. Some, like Christine, would want to remain friends but about sixty other sets of eyes would watch him walking out of McNabb's office and they would all think the same thing: what a dick.

Twelve

Rick sat there for at least forty minutes. Visions of what would happen on his return to Manchester danced shambolically through his mind like a drunk at a wedding reception. All he could see were the appalled faces of his youthful colleagues, fierce yet mocking. When he could bear it no longer, he got up and slowly carried on.

At lunchtime he opened the sandwich and was pleasantly surprised that it didn't taste awful. He walked whilst he ate and felt better for the nourishment.

The rest of the day was spent lumbering over the uneven ground until the cold started to bother him and he realised it would get dark in an hour or so. He decided it was time to call it a day; he couldn't keep up this escapade. He had to face the music and dance back to Edinburgh. He was spent, and at that particular point he didn't care what Dylan and the others would say. It was a simple matter of heading back to the road and finding the nearest town.

He switched his mobile back on. The battery was still half full, but he was correct in assuming he'd never get a signal. He came across a stretch of woodland and decided to cut through it, hoping it would be a small area and he would emerge onto a road.

Rick wandered around in the woods for some time as the sun retired. His already limited sense of direction abandoned him totally and, as there was no path, he was left stumbling through long grass as low tree branches slapped his face.

Shit, he thought, *I'm now actually lost. Only idiots and small children in fairy tales get lost in the woods.*

He started to move more quickly, shoving aside branches and desperately searching for an exit. Eventually he spied the edge of the wood and freed himself from his timber prison – but he was disappointed to see another field rather than the hoped-for road. There were no signs of animals and no fences, so presumably it wasn't a farmer's field.

Rick remembered the copy of *National Geographic* he'd skim-read in the supermarket the previous week and how inviting the Grand Canyon had looked when photographed with no tourists. Yet here he was in a country that Americans would consider the size of a large film set and he couldn't have felt more isolated.

Panic kicked in and for a moment his mind became a Boggle cube of clattering letters where thoughts couldn't fall into place coherently. Eventually he managed to pull himself together and decided to take a moment to assess the situation.

He needed to check his supplies. He slipped his bag off his shoulders and glanced at the meagre contents: one piece of flapjack and half a bottle of water. Quite what he'd expected to see in there was a mystery; it wasn't as though he had a flare gun or satellite phone.

There was only one thing for it: press on.

Crossing the field seemed to take forever. Rick tripped several times in the gathering darkness and his shoes constantly snagged boggy clumps of wet grass. Once, when he stumbled to his knees, he felt the mud seeping through his trousers. Although he couldn't see the stains, he had a vivid idea of how they would attract the attention of every passer-by once daylight came.

He was desperately miserable, and leaving the field didn't help. He couldn't see a road or a path, just a steep hill declining into yet more fields. He had that feeling you only ever have as a kid when you realise you've walked one hundred metres further from your house than you've ever done before and you start to fear you'll never see it again.

Those childhood flashbacks embarrassed him. *Surely I'm not at that point yet. What next? Is the image of a massive teddy bear chasing me going to play on repeat in my head?*

He had to keep his mind busy; he needed options,

choices to consider. He thought for a moment, but there were only three that came to mind:

Option 1 – Turn around and head back across the Swamp Thing's home.

Option 2 – Carefully make my way down the hill, trying not to slip as I go.

Option 3 – Sit down where I am and spend the night here, hoping an early morning jogger or dog walker will find my corpse.

It wasn't exactly a hard choice. There was no way Rick was going back, and he wasn't too attracted by the option of sitting around till daylight. Before the slope started, he had noticed the remains of a dry-stone wall, well-camouflaged by grass and moss, but there, nonetheless. There must be a building of some kind, somewhere Rick could shelter for the night.

Over the wall he climbed and onto the other side of it, shivering as he went. Stones littered in the grass and Rick had to be careful not to slip. It was slow going and every so often he slid back and landed on his arse; finally he sat down and crab-crawled most of the way.

The hill began to lose its steepness and eventually he started walking like a homo sapien again, but he was still hopelessly lost. He was moving through a dark valley, the grassy sides of which felt like they were closing in on him. He needed to get to higher ground.

He decided to pick up speed. The darkness blinded him. He'd been walking cautiously, but now he didn't care. He hurried on in an attempt to escape the immediate area but in his haste the inevitable happened: one of his toe caps bashed into a rock and he tripped and fell forward. His shin crunched into another rock and he yelled out in pain. For a second he was embarrassed by the cry, although he soon remembered how alone he was and that he needn't worry about looking like a wuss.

He rolled onto his back, feeling as helpless as an upturned tortoise. For a few moments he lay still and thought about sleeping the whole night right there, but eventually he sat up.

He rolled up his trouser leg to inspect the damage. By the dim light of his phone, he could see it had bruised nastily. With his wound stinging like hell, he clambered back onto his feet and carried on, limping slightly as he went.

Why did I do this? There had been many occasions when Rick had felt stupid, but he always thought that other people were more stupid than he was. Yet other people didn't run off into the unknown just because their job got difficult.

It had seemed like such a laugh when he'd left Edinburgh, but he should have realised that something like this would happen. It was obvious. You go into an area you've never been to before, in a country you hardly know and go for a walk in the woods. Suddenly Little Red Riding Hood's experiences didn't seem as far-fetched to Rick as his own.

Would it make a funny story, though? He was pretty sure that in years to come it would seem hilarious when he was doing a job he actually liked and living a life he was happy with. But he knew you didn't get the benefit of hindsight whilst the event was occurring.

After an hour he felt he'd made good progress – though progress to where, he wasn't sure – and he was sure he was far away from the torturous hill with its obstacle course of rocks. He had successfully freed himself from the valley and was now in a much flatter and more open place. The clouds had shifted and exposed the moon, and its light made choosing a path much easier.

At last he moved onto a narrow track. It wasn't exactly a B-road, and it looked barely used, but it was a road. It was so narrow he couldn't imagine that two cars could pass each other and it would be a nightmare to drive down, but he ambled along it feeling more confident that he would find civilisation soon.

Thirteen

He had been walking with his head down, trying to avoid making friends with the mud again. He stopped for a moment to catch his breath and straightened up to look at the way ahead.

And there it was.

About two hundred metres away there was a building. It was wide, with two storeys and a pole beside it with something square attached to the top. Rick could see a dim light shining through the ground-floor windows.

He could hardly believe his luck. He tried to jog towards it, but his shin was still aching and it felt like a blister had burst on his left foot; it was definitely more of a hobble than an actual jog.

As he neared the building, a fresh wave of excitement nearly drowned him. He could see what was attached to the pole: a swinging sign. It was a pub! Rick could have shouted with joy. He had found sanctuary at last – and it served beer. He no longer cared how lost he was, or that his clothes were caked in mud, or that he was in pain. He had found a pub.

As he approached the building, the sign became

clearer. He was surprised to see the image was of a lighthouse shining a beacon over a choppy sea, but at that moment he didn't care about a small detail like that. Now he knew the name of his saviour: The Light.

Pub names had always fascinated Rick. They are unique in that most businesses are named after the owner or a terrible pun, yet pub names tell a story. He looked forward to finding out from where The Light had got its name.

It was only as he crossed the car park that the name rang a bell. He shoved his hand in his satchel and pulled out the leaflet. He glanced down at the large, modern conference centre and then back up at the sturdy Edwardian public house in front of him. Despite being puzzled, he carried on towards the entrance.

Rick could hear several voices inside the pub and, through gaps in the drapes, he saw jolly-looking customers joking and swapping anecdotes.

He limped the last few steps to the vast front door. It was adorned by a large brass knocker, a bit like the haunted one on Scrooge's door. It was an effort to open it, and Rick found himself using muscles he'd no idea he possessed. He supposed that some stereotypes were still true and that people were definitely tougher north of the border.

As Rick entered a blanket of warmth engulfed him, not just in contrast to the cold outside, but because he felt it was his kind of pub. A couple of people glanced over at him while the rest of the customers got on with their evening.

There must have been about a dozen there, scattered around in twos and threes at small tables and booths. Two large men in their forties were propping up the bar, not that it needed it – it seemed sturdy enough to survive a nuclear attack should one of the world's superpowers decide that rural Perthshire was a threat to them.

When Rick approached the bar, he was thrilled to see that there wasn't a single beer or lager on draught that he recognised. He guessed they must all be from a local independent brewery. This was truly a magnificent pub. Or was it a free house? It didn't really matter.

'What can I get you, pal?' asked the landlord. His accent suggested that he was a fellow foreigner. He was around fifty, with a grey beard and a hairline that had receded several inches. Rick was relieved that he wasn't one of those older men who insisted on calling him 'lad' or 'young man'.

'I will have…' Rick said slowly, letting the words drag out of his mouth whilst he decided.

'Can I recommend Red Fox?' said one of the two men standing at the bar.

'Yes, why not? A pint of Red Fox, please.' Rick turned to thank the man, who must have enjoyed a few himself as there were several empty pint glasses in front of him. They were glasses with handles, another rarity in the franchised pubs of central Manchester.

'I haven't seen any of these beers before,' Rick told the landlord.

'No, you won't have. Judging by your accent, I'm guessing they're all new to you.' He slowly lowered the pump and Rick watched the thick brown ale flow into the glass. He took out his wallet. There was only £5 and a bit of change inside it.

'That's £2.10 please,' the landlord said, placing a full pint on a bar mat with the handle facing Rick.

Only £2.10! Is there anything this pub won't do to make me happy? Rick wondered.

After paying, he took the pint and headed over to a table by the window. He put the drink down and removed his filthy anorak. As he eased himself into a chair, his body felt grateful for the respite and he slumped back and looked out into the darkness beyond the window.

It was a full five minutes before he wrapped his fingers around the smooth glass handle and raised the pint. He drew it to his lips for a sip, savouring the refreshing taste of the creamy ale. It hit the spot like Robin Hood's arrow. Rick had never tasted such a smooth, delicious beverage in his life. *This must be why people run marathons that end at pubs,* Rick thought. *When you're tired and in agony a pint of beer is the best-tasting thing ever.*

The last few days had been an emotional marathon and he appreciated sitting back and doing nothing for a while. He was always working, or travelling to work or travelling back again. Social events were becoming scarce and even nights out with Callum didn't happen very often.

The quiet background chatter increased Rick's sense of relaxation. It was like listening to whale sounds in the bath. Despite him not being from the area, the other customers clearly held no contempt for him. He was used to burly brutes glaring at him for just walking past their locals; he'd walk, head down, past the long balconies where gangs of them would be hanging over the railing, drunk as choir boys on communion wine. Even though they rarely shouted anything out loud, Rick knew he wasn't welcome.

After emptying half the contents of his glass, Rick lumbered over to the toilets. He chose the urinal furthest from the door and relieved himself – then the moment of truth was upon him. He hadn't seen his reflection since leaving the B&B that morning. He walked slowly over to the sink and, before washing his hands, looked straight at the large mirror.

He almost laughed out loud. 'Dishevelled' was the only word that came to mind. It looked like he'd slept in a Dyson for a week. His hair was all over the place, his clothes were stained by mud and moss and his face was speckled with dirt, making it appear that he had a severe blackhead problem.

After washing his hands, he filled the sink with hot soapy water and removed his jacket. He washed his face and scrubbed off some of the mud from his trousers, not that it made much difference. He must have looked a fool when he stood at the bar and bought his drink, yet nobody had laughed. In fact, nobody seemed to have noticed. This pub was an odd sort of place, but Rick decided he liked it all the better for that.

Back at the bar, one of the two men had gone and the other was chatting to the landlord. Rick went back to his seat and slowly finished his beer. With no thoughts about how he was going to get home, he returned to the bar to waste a little more cash.

'On business are you?' asked the man who had recommended the ale. It was a miracle he was still standing; there were eight glasses in front of him, just foamy white suds remaining in them. He had clearly been on the booze all evening and the landlord had decided against collecting his empties. They were trophies to be displayed with pride.

'Not any more,' Rick replied cheerfully.

'What happened? You get the sack?' the man laughed.

Rick paused for a second and then he started to laugh too. 'Yes. Or least I will. And I couldn't care less.'

'So what are you going to do now?' The merriment in the man's voice eased slightly and he sounded more concerned.

'I honestly have no idea. Yesterday morning I was in Edinburgh, trying to sell N-ergise. I decided I'd had enough and went AWOL,' Rick explained.

'Of all the weird and wonderful stories I've heard about quitting, that has to take the biscuit,' the man said, pondering the distance Rick must have covered in the unpleasant March weather.

'To be honest, I've wanted to get out for months.' Rick's voice slowed down as he looked back at the window. As the absurdity of what had happened started to unsettle him, he suddenly couldn't concentrate on what he was saying.

'What's wrong, pal? Are you feeling ok?' The man leaned forward slightly, trying to get Rick's attention.

Rick turned to face him and a bomb of emotions exploded within him. For a fearful moment, he thought he was going to cry in front of a stranger. 'I've just realised how pointless the last few years of my life have been. I've worked at a job I hate, I've barely had a social life and I've not seen my family in ages. It's all been wasted.' He felt himself welling up.

'Cheer up, pal. It's not all that bad.' The man placed a reassuring hand on Rick's shoulder. 'Alan, get this man another beer,' he said to the landlord.

'Thank you,' Rick said weakly.

'From what you've told me, it doesn't sound like you're doing so badly.'

'How do you mean?' Rick asked, amazed that the man could see some positives in his situation.

'Well, you've been doing your job for a while now, and you've been unhappy with it for a while too. I think that says something about you.'

'Yeah, that I'm mad,' Rick sniffed.

'What's your name?'

'Rick.'

'Can I tell you a story, Rick?' All he got was a blank look in return.

Rick hadn't expected that and his distress instantly turned into confusion. *Did he actually just ask if he could tell me a story?* 'Yes, go on then,' he replied.

'There was this man from Glasgow, I forget his name. Anyway, he works late shifts most of the time and one night he comes home from work and is too tired to cook, so he decides to get a takeaway. He lives near this little kebab house, but he hasn't ever been there before.' The man had a perfect storyteller's voice. 'So this bloke goes in and looks at the menu.'

Rick suddenly thought back to the takeaway in the Edinburgh suburb. He could picture the cockroach scurrying around.

'He ends up getting a large pizza and leaves the

place thinking, okay, just this once. On his way home he's confronted by a gang of youths. Horrible thugs these lads are, real neds. They take his pizza and push him into a wall. One of them spits on him whilst the others laugh moronically. A bit shaken, the chap goes home. Now, the next day he works late again and doesn't fancy cooking so he goes back to the same takeaway and orders another pizza. On the way out the same gang of neds are waiting for him. They take their free meal and hurl a barrage of verbal abuse at him.'

The man stopped to pick up his pint. *Probably building up the suspense*, Rick thought.

'The next night the same thing happens and then again the next. This goes on for a couple of weeks. Each time the man orders a meal and each time it's taken from him by the same gang.'

'Oh, I get it. He's crazy – he puts up with something awful and doesn't complain. He's basically me, isn't he?' Rick said. This was starting to get annoying; he just wanted a few drinks, not to feature in a parable.

'Calm down. You haven't heard the end of the story. On the morning after the first pizza robbery, if you can call it that—'

'Aren't non-violent robberies a rarity in Glasgow?' Rick asked.

The man laughed loudly. 'That's better. I knew you had a sense of humour.'

The landlord hovered around listening. He'd probably heard the story before and had come over to hear the moral of the tale.

'On the morning after the first robbery, he meets a friend for coffee and tells him what happened. This friend is a hygiene inspector by trade.'

Rick smiled knowingly and so did the landlord.

'This inspector knew the takeaway the man was talking about, but it hadn't been closed down at that point.' A cheeky grin sneaked onto the raconteur's face.

'Oh, I see where this is going. What was wrong with the place?' Rick enquired eagerly.

'It had an asbestos problem. Everyone who ate there was poisoned.' The man guffawed and so did the landlord.

'I'm off for a slash,' the man said and walked away, chuckling.

Rick was dumbstruck. What kind of story was that? A happy one, or one that highlighted the massive corruption of health and safety officials? He returned to his drink; there, at least, was something he understood.

The man came back to the bar looking very cheerful. 'Hope you liked my story,' he said.

'It was interesting,' was all Rick could think to say.

'I like urban myths, especially ones with a message.'

'I must admit, I didn't really spot a message in there.' Rick felt he could be honest with this man

– even if he was still 'this man' and didn't yet have a name.

'The message I see in it is this: you can put up with a lot of shite in life, you can persevere and you can cope with things, but eventually there's a payoff. In this story it was revenge. You put up with a lot, pal, but you're still here, still standing strong. Don't worry about what might happen in the future. You'll thrive.'

The future? What is the future? Rick mused. *I don't even have anywhere to stay for the night, let alone a plan for how I might survive without a job.*

'It's nearly time, folks,' the landlord, Alan, said to the few remaining customers, who nodded and finished their drinks.

What the hell do I do now? Rick had no idea where he was and he had no means of getting anywhere. He considered asking his new friend if he could have a lift to the nearest town but felt awkward imposing on him.

Luckily, it seemed that the man had read Rick's mind. 'What are you going to do now, pal? Do you have somewhere to stay?' he asked.

'Not really. I don't even know where I am.' He didn't feel as embarrassed as he should have in revealing this.

'We're in the middle of nowhere. Or at least that's what everyone says,' the landlord chortled. He reached up for the rope attached to a brass bell and gave it a good tug. Closing time.

'I really don't know what to do now,' Rick said to his new friend. 'This is embarrassing, but could you help me?' This was a new experience; he rarely asked for anything so blatantly but he felt he could trust the man – although he decided not to mention the leaflet. He wasn't sure why; after all, it had led him to The Light.

'Of course I will, Rick,' he said merrily.

'Thank you so much. I've just realised that I've been talking to you all this time and I haven't asked your name.' As Rick was already embarrassed, this couldn't hurt.

'That's okay. It's Nathan. Nice to meet you.' He slapped a large hand on Rick's shoulder. 'I'm staying here and so should you.'

'Really? There are rooms here?' Rick hadn't realised it was a hotel as well as the best pub in the world.

Alan came round the bar and headed to a door near the toilets marked PRIVATE. 'If you would care to walk zis way, sir, I can show you to your suite,' he said in a mock-French accent.

'I don't think I can afford a room,' Rick said doubtfully.

'Don't worry about that, Rick.' Nathan winked and went to the private door.

Rick was so worn out and confused that he decided to accept what was being offered. He collected his coat and bag and followed them through to a narrow staircase that led to the second floor.

The eighteen stairs felt like Ben Nevis as Rick slowly dragged himself up them. At the summit was a carpeted landing with several doors. Between them were framed pictures. Rick was immediately reminded of the B&B he had stayed in; like the dining room there, the frames held photos of the local area and its people. Rick didn't look closely, but he saw gatherings of people in robes. Maybe the litter pickers he'd seen earlier were part of a Masonic organisation.

'You can stay in that room.' Alan pointed to a door at the far end of the corridor.

Rick could feel the magnetic pull of the bed within. 'Thank you so much for this.' He didn't sound as enthusiastic as he knew he should but he was just too tired.

Alan seemed not to notice. 'It's my pleasure. The bed is made up and the bathroom's there.' He indicated another door.

'I'll see you tomorrow morning, Rick. We can have breakfast before you leave,' Nathan said, before turning to his own room.

'Just get up whenever you want and I'll sort something out for you. Goodnight.' Alan went back to the stairs before Rick could offer further half-hearted thanks.

Inside the room, Rick threw his bag and coat onto

the bed and stripped down to his boxers. He left his clothes draped over the back of a wicker chair and slid his shoes underneath it. Then it was time to slip into the single bed and quickly drift off to sleep.

Fourteen

Another day had passed, the team had heard nothing from Rick, and Dylan was starting to get genuinely worried. He was pretty sure that no other team leader had lost anyone on a road trip before. He was in grave danger of becoming a first, and not the kind of first he wanted to be. He wanted to be the first one of McNabb's team leaders to become a CEO, not the first to go on a trip with a group of adults and lose one.

Even though Dylan liked being in charge of people, they pissed him off. He not only had to make sure his team performed well on the job but also ensure that they were happy at work, that they had their holidays sorted out, that they got on with everyone and a whole heap of other things that distracted him from selling.

The worse part of Rick's disappearing act was that Dylan knew he would have to ring McNabb. There was no way to avoid it; if he left it any longer, he would appear indecisive. He decided to do it when the team returned from the field.

As he sat in the living room, he thought he'd give Rick just one more call. He groaned loudly when he heard the toneless robot's voice telling him that the phone was switched off. He left a message. 'Look Rick, I don't know what's going on with you, but can you please call me back? Thanks.'

He wanted to say so much more. He wanted to tell Rick to grow the fuck up and come back to work, but decided that could wait.

The living room door opened and Christine walked in. She looked worn out, and Dylan reckoned that she'd been worrying about Rick. That annoyed him; Rick had caused so much bother that Dylan wanted everyone to be as furious with him as he was.

'Has he called yet?' She sat on the armchair opposite the sofa Dylan was occupying.

'No,' he answered.

'Are you going to call Daniel?' Christine knew he'd been putting it off all day.

Without answering her, Dylan picked up his phone and called his boss. 'Hi... Yes, it's been okay... Just one thing... We haven't seen Rick since yesterday morning... I don't know, he just left. He switched off his phone and we haven't heard from him since.' The next pause was longer.

Christine could feel Dylan's discomfort. He wouldn't squirm in front of her, but his face said it all.

'The only thing I can think of was a little argument we had. He lost it and shouted at me. I lost contact with him then... We tried again just now... Okay, I'll wait for it, then. Bye.' Dylan hung up and looked at Christine. After nearly a minute's excruciating silence, he said, 'He's going to have a think about it and ring us back tomorrow.'

'Was he angry?' She felt bad asking but the situation was so strange that she longed to know exactly what was happening.

'I think so. It can be hard to tell with Daniel. I've known him ages and I still sometimes can't work him out.' Dylan got up and went up to bed. He felt as if he'd earned a rest.

Fifteen

Rick found himself outdoors. The plummeting sun was streaking the sky red as he gazed around trying to fathom out where he was. For some reason he thought he was back in Manchester on one of the many streets he'd traversed over the years, but he saw no signs. The shops had no names and had boarded up windows or thick steel shutters. There was no one around, no voices to place. As he walked cautiously down the street, it was completely silent. Rick held his breath for a moment to try and pick up some sounds.

At the end of the street he came to a junction. There were vintage street signs here, but they were as blank as his mind. He had no clue what was going on or how he'd got there. He took a left and carried on along the nameless road. Now the buildings had names; they were all takeaways: *Ray's*, *Springs*, *Café Uno*. Every shop in the street was a greasy spoon, although according to the signs some of them had been awarded the coveted fourth hygiene star.

A groaning sound caught his attention. He saw four young men in tracksuits and caps writhing on the ground on the other side of the road and an abandoned burger box lying nearby. He stepped onto the road to cross the street but it looked like the ground was moving. Thousands of black creatures were scurrying along, cockroaches emerging from each shop and running onto the pothole-filled road.

Rick turned and tried to sprint back to where he'd started, but he couldn't run. He slowly dragged his feet, the top half of his body moving more quickly than his legs as he tried to swing his arms to propel himself forwards. The insects crunched nastily under his shoes as he waded through them.

The ground started to shake and the cockroaches froze. Rick heard piercing, whooshing sounds all around him. Smoke was billowing from the takeaways and cylindrical objects with pointed noses and tails of flame were whizzing through the sky. He stopped trying to run and turned on the spot.

In the distance he spotted the giant Hilton hotel that dominated the skies above Manchester. He watched as every piece of glass that covered it shattered and thousands of tiny shards drifted down onto the city below. Thousands of gallons of water gushed out from the swimming pool, and even from a great distance Rick thought he could see tiny naked men falling to their deaths.

Then the large mushroom clouds arrived all around him. By now his legs had decided to work and he started to run, faster than he'd ever run before. A searchlight beam swooped around the area, trying to focus on him. He ducked and jumped and commando rolled to avoid it.

The sky was black with smoke. Rick felt a soaring sensation as his body rose into the sky and the smoke dispersed for a while. These scenes were being repeated as far as the eye could see. Explosions were erupting all over the country, flattening buildings and churning the ground to mush, leaving only craters and the charred remains of tree stumps.

Suddenly he plummeted to the ground. His arms flailed uselessly before he landed face down in one of the fall-out filled craters. Dazed for a few seconds but unhurt, he climbed to his feet and stumbled forwards. At the rim of the crater, he saw a figure partly obscured by thick smog. As it strode straight towards Rick, he could clearly see its overly large head and floppy ears, its bulbous nose and spotted black-and-white fur.

The Dalmatian stopped a few paces from Rick and its awful, doll-like black eyes stared straight at him. Its arms rose to take hold of its ears and slowly it began to lift off its head.

Rick woke with a jolt and that slightly irrational post-dream feeling that suggested it was all real. He was confused and couldn't remember the events of the previous evening. It took about twenty seconds for him to recall the pub and his conversation with Nathan.

It had been weird but then again, running away from work into the countryside was weird and he'd done that.

Rick still had his watch on and he illuminated the dial. It was 5.30am. He spent a few seconds wondering what the dream meant before giving up and falling back into a deep sleep.

He woke again at 9.37am, instinctively checked his watch and decided that he'd successfully had a lie-in. It took him a while to get out of bed and start thinking about what he should do. He couldn't remember where the bathroom was, and he wasn't keen on the idea of searching the landing in his boxers, so he decided to get dressed and worry about washing later.

He swung his legs over the side of the bed and placed his feet on the thin rug. As he put his weight on them, he winced and dropped back. He had forgotten about the blisters that had so tormented him the previous night.

Fearing the worst, he twisted up his left leg to inspect the sole of his foot. A flap of skin about two centimetres long had ripped and folded back, exposing the pink subcutaneous layer. His right foot didn't look much better. He reached over to his bag and his plasters, keeping his body on the bed.

With his feet patched up, Rick stood up and dressed. It was a cold morning and he wasn't looking forward to the long walk back along the road. He hoped there would be some transport out there; after all, some of the customers from the night before hadn't looked fit to drive.

Rick quietly made his way back down to the bar. Alan was sitting at one of the small tables with a cup of tea and the previous day's newspaper. 'Morning. Do you want a brew?' he asked cheerfully.

'Thanks, that would be lovely.' Rick yawned.

'Nathan left about half an hour ago. He had some business to sort out,' Alan called as he headed to the kitchen.

'Does he stay here often?' Rick took a seat at the table.

'He's here quite a bit, when he's not working, that is. He never stays in one place for very long.' Alan came back whilst the kettle boiled.

'So he doesn't live here?' Rick joked.

'He lives where he wants,' Alan replied, looking nonchalantly at Rick as though Nathan deciding to live part of the time at the pub was normal. He returned to the kitchen and soon brought a large mug of tea out with a couple of plastic milk pots and several sugar sachets.

So, what now? Rick felt like saying it out loud, but didn't think Alan would be able to provide an answer. He was wrong, however; Alan knew exactly

117

what would happen to Rick next. 'You should travel a bit further north today,' he suggested.

'Really? I don't think that more trekking around the countryside is a great idea,' said Rick, surprised.

'Nathan has a nice property by a lake. He'd like it if you visited him.'

Rick stared blankly at him. *Alan must be joking. Go to yet more Nowhere to a visit a man I've only just met?*

'I'm sure it's a lovely house that he owns, but I think I should probably head back to Edinburgh. I'm not sure I can run away for much longer.' It was true; Rick knew that his daft adventure had to finish at some point.

'How are you going to get all the way back there?' It was meant to sound mischievous but Rick couldn't help spotting a flash of menace in Alan's words.

'I was hoping you'd be able to help. Is there a taxi service anywhere around here?' Rick tried to ignore how creeped-out he was starting to feel.

Alan laughed. 'No, there are no taxi services. I can't call you a limo, either.' He grinned inanely.

'What about all the punters last night? How did they get home?' Rick looked over to the front door, suspecting that he might need to make a quick getaway – but to where?

'Don't worry about that. Why don't you go to Nathan's house just for the day? Then I swear we'll make sure you get back to Edinburgh.' Alan stood up.

Rick jumped to his feet, not breaking eye contact, and the small bar stool clattered to the floor behind him. 'This just got weird. Well, *weirder*. Last night was weird, but that was in quite a pleasant way. This is just freakily weird.' His voice went up an octave on the last 'weird'.

'Calm down. I'm not going to try anything dodgy, pal.' Alan held his hands out in a show of peace.

'Right, I'm off now.' As soon as the words left Rick's mouth, he turned and bolted to the door. Thankfully it was unlocked and, with real fear motivating him to drag it open, it felt lighter than it had done when he had arrived. Less thankfully, it was bloody freezing outside.

It took about six steps before Rick realised that he'd left his jacket and anorak in the room upstairs. *Can't go back for them, no way.* He sprinted through the car park and back onto the track, his shin no longer bothering him. He didn't get very far.

Where the fuck can I go? How long will it take me to get anywhere with other people? Shit, I left my bag behind as well!

Reluctantly, he turned around and slowly walked back to The Light. Alan was standing in the doorway with his arms folded and the smug look on his face that all psychopaths must get when their prey realises that escape attempts are futile. 'I thought you might come back,' he called.

'It seems you have me by the short and curlies,' Rick said bitterly.

'Look, Rick, I really don't want to hurt you. Just come back inside and I'll explain everything.'

Rick followed the landlord back into the pub, mostly because he was cold. Alan sat down at one of the tables; he looked tired from his late shift, and Rick decided it was unlikely he would just lunge at him any second.

'So why does Nathan want to see me?' Rick demanded.

'He thinks he can help you. He knows you're unhappy and wants to show you something to perk you up.' Alan thrust both hands upwards as he said this, as if he'd had a minor electric shock.

'I really don't think he can help me. I like the man, but it sounds like he's being too optimistic.' Rick remained standing, still not sure how safe he was.

'Nathan's helped a lot of people out. Between you and me, he's offered some of them jobs.' Alan's tone was conspiratorial.

Rick's spirits perked up a bit. Maybe he was going to be offered a job. It would be something different, an escape from his current situation. *But hold on. Why am I even thinking that now? I need to focus on getting home, not accepting hypothetical jobs from potential kidnappers.*

'If you freshen up, we can leave soon. Nathan's

place is a couple of hours drive away.' Alan pointed over his shoulder to the door marked PRIVATE.

Rick stood up slowly and began to walk over to the door. 'Bathroom's first on the left. There are towels in the top cupboard,' Alan called as Rick started ascending the stairs once more.

He decided against a bath, opting for another sink scrub. Feeling refreshed, he went back down to the bar. His clothes were still stained with mud and his shirt stank of sweat, but at least he'd washed.

Alan was putting on his coat and preparing to leave. 'Right, let's get out of here,' he said excitedly.

Feeling like he had no choice, Rick slung his bag over his shoulder before following Alan out to the car park. Alan clicked his key fob and a beep came from a blue Nissan parked in the space nearest to the pub. He clambered in – but Rick didn't. He looked around once more. All he could see was empty grassland stretching in all directions.

He sighed and got into the car. As Alan reversed out of his spot, Rick got one last look at the best pub in the world.

Sixteen

Why hasn't he called yet? He said he'd call this morning. It was 11.50am and Dylan still hadn't heard from McNabb. He was making his way towards the next house on his list.

The group had decided that it was best to carry on with the day as normal, or at least Dylan had decided that. Christine had been more than happy to spend the morning in her pyjamas lounging around the mansion, waiting for a phone call. It was so cold out on the streets and, like many who grew up in sunnier climes, she despised British weather.

Dylan hadn't made any sales; he didn't feel in the groove and his usual enthusiasm and overconfidence in his abilities was somewhat lacking. *One more house and I'll have a breather.*

Knock knock. 'Hi, can I just take a moment of your time?'

'Pess off you English wanker.'

Break time. Dylan bought a weak coffee from a petrol station. His pocket buzzed as he was taking his change and he nearly ran out of the shop as if the phone inside it were a bomb. 'Hi Daniel,' he said a little too quickly.

'Hi, Dylan. Still no word from Rick?' McNabb sounded fairly calm.

'No, not heard a thing. None of us have.'

'Okay, I'm starting to get just a little bit concerned. I'm coming up there.'

Dylan didn't think he'd heard right. 'What was that?'

'I'm going to drive up to Edinburgh. I should be with you later this afternoon. I'll text you when I'm about an hour away so you can make sure you're back at the house when I arrive.' He paused, waiting for Dylan to respond. 'You hear me okay, Dylan?'

'Yes, course we'll be there. Then we can send out the search party.' The attempt at making McNabb laugh fell flat on its arse.

'Good. See you soon.'

Seventeen

As he watched the countryside fly past, Rick was reminded of the journey up to Scotland. So much had changed that it didn't seem like only four days since the trip had begun. The same time the previous week, Rick had been going through one of his usual 'I hate work' phases but now he was in a totally weird place, both geographically and emotionally. And for once it was the geographical that worried him more. He thought he should probably consider that progress.

Alan was paying more attention to the radio than the road, fiddling with the tuner, never satisfied with the station.

'Radio 1, shit. Radio 2, not much better. BBC Scotland, fuck off,' he snorted derisively. Rick wondered what he *did* like, but wasn't curious enough to ask.

The temperature had dropped even more and Rick longed to mess about with the air conditioning and feel a warm breeze on his face. When he'd been in Dylan's car, he'd had the full demonstration about how Maximus's amazing air-con system worked.

He turned to face Alan, who had given up on the radio. 'Is there any point in me asking how long it's going to take to get there?'

Alan sighed, frustrated. 'Can you stop making this sound like a kidnapping? It isn't a kidnapping!'

'Well, it feels like one.'

'It will take approximately an hour and a quarter. Happy now?'

'Not really. Are we stopping anywhere on the way? I could do with a slash.' Rick suddenly realised how badly he needed to go.

'There aren't any service stations on the way. Good thing too. They're just full of overpriced WH Smith's and...'

'Bacteria breeding ground cafés?' Rick suggested helpfully.

'Yes, exactly.'

'Seriously, I need to go soon or I'll do it all over these lovely seats.'

Alan stared at Rick angrily for a second then looked back at the road knowing he was beaten. 'I'll keep an eye out for a good spot,' he said.

Rick didn't know if Stockholm syndrome worked both ways.

Alan found a quiet B-road and pulled over. Rick opened the door to a powerful gust of wind that almost blew him onto the car roof. He hurried to the embankment and began his business. It was odd, but he felt no desire to run away – not that he could have got very far. No, the fear that he was about to be harvested for organs or have his semen stolen had passed, and he almost trusted Alan.

When he finished, Rick turned to look back at the car. Alan was looking away, no longer keen to keep playing the guard. The wind was getting stronger and Rick hurried back.

'Mission accomplished?' Alan pulled off as soon as Rick was in his seat.

'Yes. Went as well as it could have.' Rick glanced over at his strange companion.

The hour and a bit went fairly quickly for both of them and they found themselves descending into a valley of evergreen trees and greener fields. 'Nathan's house is just a few miles along this road.' Alan sounded excited.

Rick's curiosity had been building up and he too felt an unusual excitement and interest. He was about to find out exactly who the mysterious chap was who had bought him a drink and regaled him with a story. He tried to scratch off some of the stains that still flecked his trousers. Rick really didn't want to go in there looking like Worzel Gummidge's solicitor.

Whilst he was busying himself with his clothes, Alan reached over and lightly gripped Rick's forearm, shaking it slightly. Rick looked up and immediately stopped scratching.

The house that had appeared stood out against

the backdrop like a very sore thumb. The building was vast and stood three storeys high. It didn't look like a typical Scottish manor: there were no turrets, bay windows or flagpoles on the top. It didn't even look like a murder could take place there.

The house was white, with black tiles covering the roof and several skylights that made the place look like it was solar powered. The central room on the second floor had a long balcony; that must be the master bedroom. Some of the other windows had smaller balconies, and Rick could see an enormous patio at the side of the house with tables and chairs scattered across it. The garden led down to a wide lake that rippled gently in the breeze where a couple of rowing boats bobbed next to a small wooden jetty.

Alan turned into the bottom of a long drive that snaked uphill towards a gravel car park. There were two cars in front of the double garage; both looked very expensive and Rick didn't recognise the makes.

As Alan's tyres crunched on the gravel, the front door opened. Nathan's large, wrestler-like frame emerged and sauntered over to the car. He was dressed very differently to how he had been at the pub. Gone was the thick green fleece and faded jeans; instead he wore a suit, the kind that Rick had seen on several of the senior managers in the Mercury Group. It was charcoal grey, double breasted and had been tailored to fit his body perfectly. His blue-and-white striped tie was tied in a Windsor knot and secured by a platinum tie pin.

Alan and Rick got out and walked over to their host.

'Great to see you again, Rick.' Nathan shook his hand warmly.

'Thanks for the invite.' *I think*.

'It's a pleasure. There's so much I want to explain to you. This way, please.' He indicated to the front door.

The interior of the house was as impressive as the outside suggested. There was a large circular hall with a staircase that spiralled around the wall and up to the second floor. In the centre was a mosaic of the regimental badge of the 5th Highland Rifles, a throwback to Nathan's military days. The fierce stag's face in its centre glared up at Rick, reminding him how out of his depth he was.

'Please come through to the drawing room.' Nathan led Rick towards an open door. Alan didn't react and Rick assumed he'd been here a few times before.

'I bet you've never been in a drawing room like this that didn't have a velvet rope across the furniture,' Nathan said, laughing.

'I'm going to have to agree with you on that one,' Rick replied.

The room did look like it was straight out of Pemberley, which was odd since the outside of the house was so modern. The floor was covered in a large red rug with golden swirls emblazoned around the edges. There were portraits of historic figures on the wall, some of whom Rick could recognise and others who looked like generic military types and old Scottish lairds.

He wandered over to a ten-foot-high portrait of Napoleon, suddenly realising his shoes were filthy. 'Oh God, I'm sorry. I've ruined the rug.' Never having been invited into a private stately home before, Rick was unsure of the shoe-taking-off etiquette. There was a trail of faint muddy footprints going straight across the expensive crimson floor covering.

'Don't worry, it'll clean up.' Nathan was more interested in Rick's reaction to the room as he turned on the spot, taking it all in.

There were chaise longues parallel to the walls and a rustic oak coffee table in the centre of the room. One wall was covered with a large bookcase that reminded Rick of McNabb's office back in Manchester. There was even a brass globe in the corner that Rick was convinced must be full of bottles of brandy and port. Despite the difference in size between this and Vaughn's house in Edinburgh, he had to admit they had a similar style: classical rich meets very new money.

'Take a seat. The others will be here shortly.' Nathan sat down in a large armchair.

'Others?'

'There are some people I'd like you to meet. We'd like to help you out,' Nathan said enthusiastically.

'I really appreciate all this, but I'm still confused as to why.' Rick looked away, feeling embarrassed.

'I should explain that we have a mutual friend.'

Rick looked back at him. It didn't take long for the penny drop. He didn't know many people who could be mates with a millionaire. 'Daniel McNabb?' he asked.

'Got it in one. We go way back.'

Rick thought Nathan Vaughn was about the same age as McNabb and presumably came from Aberdeen. 'You work for the Mercury Group?' He already knew the answer.

'We were there in the early days. Daniel and I were the first team leaders that Tessa Jansen appointed. They were great times. We were all ambitious – too ambitious, some thought. We wanted the world and every luxury it could afford. As you can see, we mostly got what we wanted.' Leaning back, he indicated the room.

'Mostly? It looks like you've got everything any-one could dream of,' Rick said, not bitterly.

'We're not just *anyone*, Rick. It seems like you don't understand that.' Nathan sounded mildly exasperated.

'That's the type of thing my team leader says. He doesn't think I get it, either.'

Nathan shot forward in his seat as though Rick had said something fascinating and he wanted to know more. 'What is it you don't understand? You've been doing this for years and you've seen how others have done really well. What is it you don't understand?'

'Well, it's just...' Rick paused. He really didn't know where to start. 'Have you ever been with a group of people where they all think one thing, or believe one thing, and you don't? Even though you're part of that group, you still don't believe in it?' was the best he could come up with.

Nathan clasped his hands together and looked up in exaggerated thought. 'Yes,' he said finally. 'Yes, I know what you mean. I wasn't the brightest when I was at school and could never understand why all my teachers told me to work hard in class. Education seemed so pointless then.' He looked back at Rick hopefully, thinking they had made a breakthrough.

Rick wasn't so sure. A lot of the kids at his school thought like that. 'Well, I suppose I feel a bit like that school kid at work. Everyone really wants to sell and I can see why because they make a lot of money. But I just don't want to do what they do.'

'And it's hard to change jobs at the moment,' Nathan said. 'So you stuck it out – until you went

AWOL, that is.' He sniggered slightly, not sure if it was too early to joke about that.

Rick laughed. 'That about sums it up. Am I weird for thinking like that? Do you think I'm throwing away a good opportunity?' He felt good talking to someone who understood his world but who didn't work with him. He could talk to Callum about his job, but he knew Callum never fully understood.

'I think you're in a good position at the moment, Rick. This is a crossroads for you, a chance to choose where you want to go in life.'

'I've really no idea where to go. I know I don't have a job any more, but in a way that's a good thing. I can find something completely new.' Rick meant what he said, even though he'd blown his chances of getting a good reference.

The two men sat in silence for a few minutes. The sound of a door closing In the hall caught Rick's attention. He'd forgotten about Alan and the oddness of their journey to the mansion. *When am I going to get back home? Back to some form of normality?*

'You haven't necessarily lost your job.' Nathan's sudden words nearly made Rick jump.

'Haven't I?' Surely running away from work wasn't exactly grounds for promotion.

'I'm good friends with your boss, remember. I can put in a good word. Maybe it's just the office you're in, or your team leader.'

'So you think I should move?' Rick was even

more surprised.

'If you had a new start in a different city it might help. There are Mercury Group offices all over the country – Liverpool, Sheffield, Nottingham, Leeds – or you could go further afield. There's always the Edinburgh office,' Nathan suggested.

'I really don't think that would help. Those offices will be full of the same type of people, just with slightly different accents. I need a complete change.' Rick stood up; he wanted to pace around a bit but he saw his footprints on the rug and thought better of it. He sat back down.

'But it would be a change. I can show you something different. Different, but integral to our business.' Nathan looked deadly serious.

Rick didn't want to know. He wanted a proper new start.

'A few colleagues are coming around later this afternoon. They're all heavy hitters in the Mercury Group. We want to show you exactly why we are so successful. Trust me. If you want to be successful you can be, Rick. I want to show you how.'

Rick sighed. *I give up.* 'Okay, Nathan. Show me what you need to show me.'

Eighteen

Dylan sat calmly in one of the armchairs in Vaughn's living room. He didn't feel as stressed out as he had done earlier that morning. It wasn't his fault Rick had left. So they had argued – Rick was the one acting like a petulant child. Dylan believed he had handled things appropriately, although he was still annoyed that he'd been out for nearly four hours and hadn't a single sale to his name. That was unheard of. Rick had really messed up his day and he planned on telling him so when he returned.

Christine and Jamie were sitting with him. Jamie hadn't sold anything that day either and was starting to wonder whether he was in the right line of work. He dreaded the next conversation with his dad.

The sound of a car in the drive broke the silence. Dylan jumped up and hurried over to the window. Glancing out, he saw one of Daniel McNabb's fleet, a black Range Rover.

The man himself got out and looked at the house, smiling to himself at his memories of the place, of when Nathan Vaughn and he had first seen it whilst selling in the area. Vaughn had said he would own it one day. His reminiscing over, McNabb headed for the front door and rang the bell.

Christine went to answer it whilst Dylan stayed by the window, wondering exactly what he was going to say after, 'Hi Daniel.'

'Hiya, great to see you.' Christine's usual zeal was still very present.

'It's wonderful to see you too, Christine. Even if the circumstances aren't so wonderful,' McNabb said. He followed Christine into the living room and greeted Jamie and Dylan. 'So how's your first road trip been?' he asked Jamie.

'Good thanks,' Jamie replied, not too convincingly.

'Glad to hear it,' McNabb said, before turning to Dylan. 'So team leader, tell me exactly how you lost a team member.'

Dylan was speechless and just stared at him.

'I'm kidding, Dylan. No need to look so scared.' McNabb laughed and sat on the large sofa.

It didn't take Dylan long to explain how the week had gone: Rick's comments to Jamie; his sudden development of a bad temper; his attitude, and flipping at his team leader on the estate.

McNabb listened carefully, his face betraying no emotion, whilst his three employees all tried to gauge how full of rage he was. After Dylan's tale ended there was silence for a moment, then McNabb spoke. 'This is an odd turn of events. I always knew Rick wasn't as keen on his job as the rest of you, but to run away like that? That's a surprise. Maybe it's my fault. Perhaps I shouldn't have sent him here with you,' he said thoughtfully.

Dylan stiffened in his chair and Christine shot him a look. Was he trying to supress a retort? She knew he wouldn't want to openly criticise his boss, but she also knew that the comment McNabb made was as much a dig at Dylan as it was at himself. She decided to steer the conversation away from blame and back to Rick. 'I hope he's alright. I mean, anything could have happened to him.'

McNabb smiled slyly, as though he knew something the others didn't. 'Don't worry about his wellbeing. He's in incredible comfort right now,' he said.

'What? What's going on?' Dylan asked excitedly.

McNabb stood up and walked over to the drinks cabinet. He was in no hurry to enlighten them. 'Vaughn always had such poor taste in whisky. I mean, Whyte and MacKay! He drinks like a jakey!' he said, proud that his natural dialect hadn't completely betrayed him since moving to England.

His three underlings looked at him, confused. He turned to them and sighed. 'I had a call from Nathan Vaughn whilst I was on my way up here. He's with Rick now.' Still the looks of confusion. 'Rick arrived at Nathan's Highland home this morning.'

Dylan couldn't work out if this was a joke or not. Subtle humour was never his thing. 'How the hell did that happen? He doesn't know Vaughn. He doesn't know where he lives.' He was genuinely hurt that Rick knew someone higher up in the business that he didn't.

'He met Nathan due to some unusual circumstances yesterday evening. Nathan took quite a shine to him and invited him to his home.' McNabb had to laugh at the priceless look on Dylan's face.

'So, we just have to wait for him to come back. We can carry on selling,' Dylan said hopefully.

'Not yet. I want to make sure Rick's definitely back and not going to pull another Lord Lucan on us. Get your coats, we're off.'

The team still stared back at him. Finally Christine laughed. 'Really? A road trip within a road trip?'

'One of our team is missing. It's time for him to come in from the cold.'

Nineteen

It was heavenly to have a good soak. Rick had been in the large bath for nearly an hour and felt as though he could fall asleep in it. The tub was the size of a Jacuzzi and could probably take six people. The bathroom was bigger than Rick's flat and mostly made of marble. Two large windows looked out onto the vast football-pitch lawn, similar to the one at Vaughn's Edinburgh home. It was an odd feeling for Rick to be in a bathroom without frosted windows – but who could watch you here when you were in the nip? A pervy gardener with some binoculars?

Rick's clothes were in the wash. After drying himself, he reached for a thick cotton dressing gown, which he intended on keeping on for as long as he could. Glancing through the medicine cabinet, he found a small green box labelled *Compeed*. He recognised these as blister plasters; he'd used them before and decided to apply them again, just in case there was more walking to be done. It was a decision he wouldn't regret.

It was 1.30pm when he went down to the kitchen. He was hungry, and assumed Vaughn's hospitality would extend to lunch.

'Your clothes should be out of the drier in about an hour.' Vaughn looked up from his broadsheet newspaper as Rick entered the room.

'Thanks. That bathroom is amazing, by the way. Well, the whole house is.'

'You like it, then? You never know what sort of house you might end up living in.'

'One can but hope,' Rick said in a mock-posh voice.

'You can, you certainly can. I'm so excited about this afternoon. I just got a text from Paul Jackson. He's on his way,' Vaughn said.

Rick had only seen Paul Jackson on that one occasion at the conference centre. Jackson had annoyed him, and the thought of spending an afternoon with him wasn't the most appealing prospect. But Vaughn was so enthusiastic, it was hard not to get caught up in the euphoria.

They had lunch together in the large kitchen. Vaughn was a decent cook and made a delicious tuna pasta bake. Afterwards Rick got dressed; it felt so good to be in clean clothes after spending two days getting muddier than a farmer.

At around 4pm, people started arriving. First there was Tessa Jansen. She marched into the lobby to be met by a childishly excited Vaughn. 'It's so good to be here, Nathan,' she said after kissing him on the cheek. She hadn't changed dramatically since Rick had last seen her. She was still in her early forties and still had greying hair tied back in a bun.

'There's a young chap I'd like you to meet, Tessa. One of Daniel's minions.' Vaughn indicated Rick.

'Pleased to meet you. I'm guessing you do have a name and that Nathan's just shit at introductions,' she said.

'God, I'm sorry. This is Rick,' Nathan added and Tessa shook Rick's hand.

'Good to meet you too,' Rick said, surprised at how convincing he'd made himself sound. It felt strange to meet her face to face; last time he'd been one person in a vast crowd of adorers.

The next to arrive was Paul Jackson, who turned up in a predictably expensive car and was introduced in a similar manner to Tessa. He looked keen and wide-eyed, despite having just driven a considerable distance.

'Now we're just waiting for Nigel,' Nathan explained as everybody settled into comfy chairs in the drawing room.

The big shots talked shop for a while and Rick pretended he was following the conversation. It was odd for him to hear what rich people chatted about in their down time. It turned out they talked about money but it didn't seem vulgar; it just seemed normal, as though they were a group of students discussing the merits of daytime TV.

Cities were mentioned. Jackson had just got back from Tokyo, and Vaughn sounded like he was planning on expanding into Madrid. New cars were discussed. The cost of university abroad was already on Tessa's mind, despite her eldest only being twelve.

Then Nigel arrived. Rick had expected him to be another Paul Jackson, a middle-aged, boring man who had probably crossed a time zone at some point that day. But he didn't even arrive in the same type of expensive car as the others; in fact, he didn't even seem to arrive by vehicle at all. There was no crunch of gravel on the driveway and definitely no shudder of propeller blades over the house. There was just a loud, thudding knock on the door which made everyone jump.

There was silence for a few seconds. Vaughn composed himself first. 'That must be the final member of the famous five. I'll go let him in.' He jumped up and went into the hallway.

'It's alright, I'll get it.' Alan's voice drifted through to the drawing room. Rick wondered if he was disappointed not to be one of the 'famous five'.

'Greetings all!' came a slightly shrill older voice. 'Nathan, it's been too long, sir. And Alan, the last time I saw you I was looking up at you from the floor of your fine inn,' he recalled.

'Yes, you'd had a few then. I'm not surprised that's all you can remember,' Alan said.

'Where're the rest of those capitalist buggers?' Nigel spoke with a slight northern accent, although it was one that had influences from many areas. He was like an old-fashioned salesman who'd spent his professional life driving round Britain before settling into a head-office job.

'In there. We have a new member for the group,' Nathan explained.

Rick's ears pricked up. *New member? Did I agree to that? I thought I was just meeting some rich people so Vaughn could make a point.* He looked to the door, not quite expecting what happened next

Nigel burst into the room like a magician on a Vegas stage. He was wearing a long black cloak attached at the neck by a gold four-leaf clover. He held his arms aloft to reveal a tracksuit and trainers beneath his unusual coat. The trainers were slightly muddy and, in a rare moment of playing detective, Rick deduced that he must have walked at least part of the way to the house.

Nigel must have been around sixty years old but looked fit; his face, adorned by a magnificent walrus moustache, seemed to gleam. Rick thought he vaguely recognised him, but couldn't for the life of him think where he'd seen him before.

'Tessa, Paul, it's a delight to see you both again,' Nigel said enthusiastically. He turned to Rick. For a second, he looked surprised then his shock turned to merriment and he theatrically extended his hand. 'May I have the pleasure of asking your name, young man?' He took Rick's hand and shook it lightly.

'I'm Rick. I'm...' He really didn't have a clue how to describe himself. Was he a friend of the group he had only just met?

Thankfully Nathan stepped back into the room and saved him. 'Rick's from the Mercury Group. I thought he might like to see how it's run,' he said.

See how it's run? Surely that happens in an office, not someone's house.

Nathan seemed to guess what Rick was thinking. 'You'd be surprised to see how differently we do things compared to other national corporations.'

'Oh yes, it really is unique. And you're the lucky chap who gets to see what's behind it all,' Nigel proclaimed.

'Now that we're all here, let's have some scran.' Nathan beckoned the group to follow him through the lobby and into a large dining room where Alan was busy with cutlery and napkins. Wine glasses were out, and Rick counted at least four different types of knife. Thinking he'd just stepped into an officer's mess scene from a colonial war film, he was afraid he'd be fined if he used the lobster-killing knife on his bread roll.

They all took seats. Nathan uncorked the wine bottle and began pouring. Alan came back with a serving trolley loaded with six plates. He put one in front of each guest and the final one at his own place. Smoked salmon wasn't something Rick would have considered ordering at a restaurant, but he was surprised how much he liked it.

'This is lovely, Alan. You should have a gourmet night at The Light,' Nathan said after only one mouthful.

'I'm not sure if gourmet would go down too well with the regulars,' Alan scoffed.

'They travel far enough to get there, you'd think they appreciate it,' Tessa pointed out. 'Or are the taxi fares too much to afford a bite to eat?'

After the starter Alan collected the plates and went to get the main course of lamb escalope with sweet potatoes, carrots and spinach. As they ate, Nathan explained how he had first met Nigel. 'I was twenty-five at the time and I hadn't been in the business long,' he began.

'Yes, you were quite the whippersnapper,' Nigel pointed out.

'Everyone in the Edinburgh office had heard the name Nigel Winters, but I didn't know anyone who'd seen him in the flesh. I was just a rep on the streets trying to sell N-ergise.' Nathan reached over for the bottle of wine to top up his glass.

Rick wondered how long this one was going to be. In the last couple of days he'd had story time on more occasions than when he'd been at primary school.

'I was sent by Tessa to a small town several miles away. I didn't understand why – there were only sixty houses on the list that we could sell to. They were traditional folk, and some still bought coal for open fires. Yet there I was with two others, my team leader, Simon, and another rep, Casey. We didn't feel hopeful.'

It surprised Rick that other salesman in their company ever had doubts. They all seemed more positive than the inventor of Prozac.

'Anyway, I wasn't having a good day so I took a break. It was only meant to be for an hour, but I got a bit lost. I found myself deep in the countryside and miles away from anything. Eventually I came across a pub.'

'Best pub in the country,' Nigel said.

Alan shrugged and looked a little embarrassed, as if to say, 'I try.'

Rick stopped eating for a second, not believing what he was hearing. 'Let me guess. When you were at your lowest ebb, you stumbled across The Light and were told an uplifting, if slightly ambiguous, story by a wise stranger,' he blurted out.

For a moment everyone around the table looked shocked then they burst into hysterical laughter.

'Then they laugh at you, right?' Rick fired this one at Paul, who doubled over. 'What is all this about? Can I just get a simple answer?' He raised his voice this time.

The laughter died down. Nathan straightened up and held up a hand to signal Rick to calm down. 'I'm sorry. We shouldn't laugh. I just didn't expect that from you,' he said, trying to supress a mini-laugh unsuccessfully.

'It wasn't just a pub. There was a God-awful eyesore of a building site behind it,' Alan said indignantly.

'Oh, come now, it wasn't that bad, Alan,' Nigel snapped, leaning forward in mock menace.

Nathan, who was sitting next to Nigel, placed a hand on his shoulder and lightly pushed him back. He turned to Rick. 'The Light was envisaged as a large complex, expanding well beyond the ancient pub,' he explained. 'We realised eventually that it wasn't financially viable to have a large conference hall so far away from any big towns.'

'But the MD at the time was mad,' Nigel said, pointing both his index fingers at himself.

'Yet you still print the leaflets.' Rick remembered that the one in his bag was definitely not made in the 1980s.

'We found they were useful, very useful for enticing young reps to be a little more intrepid whilst out on road trips.' Nigel sounded proud at having thought up the plan .

'What about the name and the picture of the lighthouse?' Rick was determined that his interest in pub names would be indulged.

'Ah, yes. My idea again,' Nigel explained. 'It's a beacon to show the way to success, but it only shows the way to a very specific group of people. After all, a real lighthouse would be no use to a butcher or a taxidermist,' he concluded pompously.

'I suppose that makes some sense in a way,' Rick said, thinking it best just to agree.

'If this seems strange now, wait until we go outside,' Tessa said, giggling.

'Go outside? What the hell are you on about?' The frustration was too much for Rick. He felt his head was going to self-destruct.

'Don't worry, I will explain it, Rick,' Nathan said. 'But before I do, I've got to say I'm not joking about any of this. I honestly did meet Nigel at The Light, and everything that followed was as a result of that. He talked to me and he inspired me to have bigger ambitions than I ever had before.'

'There are other secrets behind our success. It isn't just a positive mental attitude that does it,' Nigel said.

'I wasn't just told to picture my goals and dream big. Nigel let me in on the whole thing,' Nathan continued.

'I don't just work for the Mercury Group. I'm on the board of directors for N-ergise.' Nigel let that hang for a moment.

Rick looked at him blankly, wondering if this was an incredible revelation or not.

'That might not seem like an incredible revelation, but it has guaranteed the success of the Mercury Group,' Nigel said smugly.

'How's that?' Rick thought he might as well ask.

'We have found a way to ensure that N-ergise is the most successful energy provider in Britain. You may have noticed that all our competitors are dwindling at the moment.'

Rick could vaguely remember a *Guardian* article a few weeks previously that claimed that N-ergise was steaming ahead. He'd been very disappointed; it meant his job was secure.

'Eventually we'll be the only one, Rick.' Paul reached forward to grab the wine bottle. He was the only one who had filled each glass right up to the rim.

'Is that some kind of hostile takeover?' Rick asked, impressed with himself for using a phrase like that. Everyone around the table laughed but this time it was more pleasant, as if Rick were in on the joke.

'You'd have to be barking to pull off something like that,' Nigel said.

Barking!

'Woof woof,' Nigel held his hands out like paws and waggled his tongue at Rick.

'That was you at the conference?' Rick certainly had never expected that the man in the suit had literally been 'top dog'.

Twenty

The Range Rover was spacious and comfortable, and McNabb was a very experienced driver. He drove speedily but, unlike with Dylan, his passengers didn't feel like they were being given a lift by Mr Toad.

Christine was in the front, despite Dylan's protests at having called shotgun. She found a breezy local radio station and they spent the journey listening to nostalgic music from a time most of them didn't remember.

'I wish I'd been born ten years earlier. I'd have been a proper eighties' child,' Christine said.

'What was so good about the eighties?' Dylan's moment of meek quietness had passed.

'It looks great in all those music videos. The fashion was funky and the people were all a bit weird. I'd have fitted right in.'

'I hate to burst your bubble, but the 1980s really weren't that great.' McNabb raised his eyebrows slightly as he thought back to a time of strikes and unemployment. He felt all the more grateful that he had succeeded in business after hearing such a ridiculous comment.

'Don't spoil it! I bet you had a right laugh,' Christine shrieked, before starting a discussion about how much better TV presenters' hairstyles were back then.

Twenty-one

After the meal, the group retired to the drawing room for brandy. Rick had already had two large glasses of wine with the food and was feeling drowsy. Paul downed his in one and was pouring another glass when Nathan spoke up. 'I think we should head up to the altar before nightfall.'

'Indeed, indeed. The time is nigh,' Nigel chirped.

The others nodded whilst Rick tried to imagine what the hell the altar was.

'I'm going to get changed. We'll set off in ten.' Nathan drained his glass and went into the hall. When he returned, Rick was surprised to see that he was wearing a similar robe to Nigel's. He was carrying two more over his arm, presumably for Paul and Tessa.

'Are you all Freemasons or something?' Rick asked.

Nathan gave a derisive snort. 'We're nothing like them. You know, they aren't even secretive these days. Their headquarters display a public logo.'

Rick wasn't sure why that was such a bad thing. With everyone but him robed up, the group walked onto the gravel drive. It was 7pm and darkness was just beginning to fall. As they walked at a leisurely pace towards a small path, Rick turned to look back at the grand house. Alan was standing in the doorway watching them leave. He didn't wave; he merely shook his head and closed the door.

A sudden chill shot through Rick. He didn't quite know why, but he felt sure he wouldn't see the house again.

There was silence as they walked and even Nigel seemed unusually subdued. The path took them past the lake and outside the grounds through a moss-covered gate that wouldn't have looked out of place in *The Secret Garden*. It was wide enough for them to walk two abreast, with Paul and Tessa taking the lead and muttering to each other as they went. Nigel and Nathan followed them, with Rick bringing up the rear.

He realised that he'd never been in as many situations where he thought he should run as during the last few days. He wasn't keen on running and hated the feeling of sweat dribbling down his back and around his crotch. And even if he'd been Sebastian Coe, he had nowhere to run to. He was somewhere in Scotland and didn't know how to get back.

For the first time, he wondered what he would do when he got home. Not in an employment sense because he knew he'd lost his job, but what would he say about what had happened after he went

AWOL? Would anyone believe a word of it? He doubted it. He suspected he'd have to spend much of his life trying to forget about it to avoid looking odd.

He decided he'd tell Callum so at least the whole experience would give someone a laugh. Obviously Christine knew he'd disappeared, so he figured he could tell her. The idea of trying to explain to his family and other friends was excruciating.

After a short walk, the path ascended to a copse of trees. They trudged in silence, apart from Nigel who jogged ahead with a spring in his step. Rick half expected him to jump up and click his heels.

At the top of the hill, they made their way through the trees. Rick remembered the last time he'd tried to navigate through a wood and kept his eyes on his feet, watching out for trip hazards. When he emerged at the other side, he gasped at the sight that greeted him.

The hill they had climbed had a flat top, like a miniature Table Mountain. They were confronted by a large circle of huge rocks, each one at least four-metres high, weather beaten, gnarled and topped by jagged points. In the centre was another shorter but wider boulder that resembled a stone bed. The stones looked like an army of knights standing to attention around a lazy, inebriated king.

Rick stood, rooted to the spot, trying to take it in. The place hadn't been visible from the house due to the trees, but for some reason Rick felt he recognised it.

The others walked into the circle and headed towards the central rock. 'Welcome to the Devil's Altar!' Nigel called out merrily.

Nathan turned to Rick. 'Isn't it exquisite?' he asked.

'It's certainly not what I expected,' was all Rick could say.

'You must have seen others like it,' Paul called out. 'There are loads of these all over Britain.'

'Yeah, but I've never seen one in the flesh. Or the rock.' Rick tentatively followed them into the circle. The wind was starting to pick up and Rick couldn't work out if he was shivering because of the cold or through a sense of fear. *It's the cold, of course it is. They're just stones. Really big stones!*

Nigel bounded onto the bed-like stone and stood proudly, raising his hands to address the small gathering. 'These stones date back to around 2,300BC, or some time in the Neolithic age. The circle was later used by Druids, but we use it now,' he proclaimed.

'Use it for what? They're just a load of rocks,' Rick shouted up at him, trying to be heard over the howling wind.

Nigel looked genuinely hurt. 'My dear boy, they are so much more than just rocks!'

'This location is the key to what we do. Our

company thrives because of it,' Tessa claimed.

'It's the secret to our success,' Paul said with slightly less enthusiasm. He too was shivering and clearly wasn't enjoying being outdoors as much as the others.

'But how?' Rick wondered aloud.

'It's all about energy – or should that be N-ergise? These megalithic sites are a source of electromagnetic energy.' Nathan was slowly approaching Rick as he spoke. 'I won't bore you with the ins and outs of how, but suffice to say they provide completely renewable energy to most of the country.'

For some reason Rick felt this wasn't complete bullshit, though he wasn't sure why. Maybe it was the area's atmosphere, but something about it seemed like it could indeed produce energy.

'The other companies are dying at the moment. They can't compete with us.' Nigel jumped down from his perch and landed awkwardly. 'I've made sure that the Mercury Group has full control of this site. I told you I'm on the board of directors at N-ergise and I've made the company you work for thrive, the same company I helped set up. I've made salespeople rich, Rick. I just wish you could appreciate that.' He sounded mildly frustrated.

Rick didn't respond because he needed a few minutes to gather his thoughts. As he walked over to the central stone, the taller ones started to feel like gaolers incarcerating him on the Devil's Altar.

The others watched him patiently.

Eventually he worked out what he needed to say. 'This is very impressive.' The rest of the group nodded. 'But I don't think it'll sway me, if that is the point of this visit. I've seen others get rich and successful. I've seen the sports cars and the holiday snaps. I've heard the endless stories of what people have done with their money, or what they're planning to do with it. I think this has just confirmed everything I think I already knew.'

He paused, suddenly aware of how much they were hanging onto his every word. 'That is,' another pause for dramatic effect, 'that rich people are just plain weird.'

There was silence for a few seconds. The wind died down and nobody spoke. Rick expected another round of riotous laughter like at dinner but, worryingly, none came. 'I'm not really sure what happens now. I take it you've done this before, brought future best sellers here to see how it's all done?'

'Yes, Rick, we have. And every one of them who left here went on to be a key player in the business,' Nathan explained.

'Tell him what happened to the ones who didn't leave,' Nigel piped up excitedly.

This time they all laughed.

Rick chuckled. 'Didn't leave! What happened? Did the ghosts of ancient Druids sacrifice them? Or was the energy from the circle so powerful it sent them into orbit?'

'Oh Rick, you really have no idea what we do.' Tessa forced herself to stop laughing in order to speak.

'Well, you haven't told me. All I've heard is a load of mysterious talk and cryptic bullshit,' Rick shouted, much to the delight of the others who continued to laugh.

Nathan motioned to the group to quieten down. 'Yes, he's right. I'll say something less cryptic to you now.' He paused. 'We're going to kill you.'

Everyone fell completely silent.

'Why? Why are you going to kill me?' Rick wasn't sure if they were joking or not, but he could feel beads of cold sweat running down his neck and forehead.

'Does someone have to have a reason to kill?' Paul asked nonchalantly.

'Normally, yes.' Rick started to edge slowly backwards.

'You're not normal, Rick,' said Nathan, his long cloak billowing menacingly as he advanced towards his protégé of the last twenty-four hours.

'We showed you our world and you rejected it.' Nigel was making an arc round to Rick's right.

'You have to appreciate that this is all top secret,' Paul added.

'Yes, we can't let you leave.' Tessa threw back one

side of her cloak, revealing a long dagger in a silver-and-green patterned scabbard attached to her belt. She slowly drew it out; the blade looked dull in the gathering darkness but no less threatening. Together with the rest of the group, she advanced towards their victim and passed the dagger to Nigel, who took it by the hilt.

'You're all mental.' Rick moved faster. His calves hit the side of the altar and he fell backwards onto the vast stone.

'I'm not going to enjoy this. I really thought you'd go for it, mate.' Nathan still sounded as genial as he had back at The Light.

It struck Rick that it was at the pub where he'd seen this place before. The photos on the landing featured people wearing long robes, and in the background he had seen blurred grey images. They must have been the stones and the robed figures of the energy salespeople of yesteryear.

'Come, comrades, let us complete this task,' Nigel cried.

Apart from Vaughn, they all advanced towards Rick. He placed both hands at his sides on the rock and shoved himself up, the extra thrust throwing him forward and giving him a minor head start as he fled back towards the trees.

Vaughn remained stationary, his complacency shining like a searchlight over his seemingly doomed escapee.

Rick didn't turn to look back. His pursuers were all older than him and were still wearing the long thick cloaks, giving him an advantage. But, unlike them, he had no clue where he was going. Tearing through the trees, Rick thought about going back to the house but he assumed Alan was involved. Oh God, what now?

Twenty-two

McNabb's Range Rover hadn't even stopped when the doors were flung open by its occupants. Everyone was cramped and tired; the excitement of the 'road trip within a road trip' had died down fairy quickly and boredom had set in. Christine's attempt to raise morale with a rendition of 'The Wheels of the Overpriced Car Go Round and Round' had not succeeded.

They were in a small petrol station that looked like it was stuck in the 1960s. The pumps still had flick dials although the petrol was more expensive than it was in that era. Not that it mattered to McNabb.

The others hurried into the shop to stock up on snacks and drinks because none of them knew how long they would be on the road. McNabb took his phone and looked for the number for Vaughn's Highland manor. He was surprised to see a no-mobiles sign on the pump and decided to ignore it, figuring it was hardly likely to cause a mini-Chernobyl.

After several rings, he heard Alan's voice on the line. 'Hi, Alan? It's Daniel here. How are you?' he asked.

'I'm very well, thanks. Yourself?' Alan replied cheerfully.

'Nay bad, nay bad. Is Nathan there?' McNabb thought he'd get straight to the point.

'You've just missed him. He went up to the circle with some of your lot and the new lad.'

McNabb felt his chest tighten. The circle! Why take Rick there? Did that mean that Rick had had a change of heart for some reason? Had he decided he could become one of them? Was he even given a choice? Deep down McNabb had felt a nagging sensation that Rick would leave Gold Force at the end of the trip; the only real explanation was that they'd decided that, in the absence of Dylan, Rick would do. It was completely off script.

Then again, maybe Rick had embraced their ways... No, that was not what had happened at all! Nathan had gone too far this time.

Twenty-three

It had been a particularly long day for Daniel McNabb when he'd arrived at his apartment the previous Tuesday night. He had been at the office since 8.30am and had only called it quits at 9.40pm. He had driven home robotically, not taking in his surroundings, and by the time he approached the building he wanted nothing more than a glass of Scotch and to sit on his luxurious leather sofa listening to Radio 2. But he knew he couldn't; that night he had a lot to think about.

The road trip was approaching. As he parked his Audi in the car park of his apartment block, McNabb knew he had to finalise the plan. He also had to choose someone for the task.

He remembered his own initiation. That too had been during a road trip, and it was there that he had met Nigel who had shown him a world he could never have imagined. It was then that McNabb went from being an average salesman to something special. He had stood at the Devil's Altar and been told by Nigel to soak up the atmosphere. It felt amazing. Daniel understood there was something significant about the location, although he'd never quite been able to put it into words.

Walking through the car park that made up the ground floor of his apartment block, he laughed at his moment of revelation being referred to as 'soaking up the atmosphere'. It made it sound like no more than a weekend break in Tuscany.

As he ascended the lift to the top floor, he remembered that he had stayed in a small chalet near the site. It wasn't quite as impressive as the large mansion Vaughn had eventually built, but it had been a good time despite a certain feeling of lost innocence that McNabb hadn't experienced since he first left home to join the army at sixteen.

He entered his penthouse apartment with a sense of relief, like a bear returning to its den for hibernation. His property consisted of one very large multi-purpose living space with two bedrooms, a bathroom and a cupboard stuffed with various articles of barely-used sports clothing and equipment. He often tried out these sports when abroad but found he tired of them when he returned to his normal British life.

The living room was dominated by two large sofas with a glass coffee table between them. It was designed for conversation between guests, whose first comments were usually, 'Where's the TV?' McNabb didn't watch a lot of television and only had a small set in his bedroom.

One wall of the lounge had a vast bookcase

for his extensive record collection and books about business strategy. The two external corner walls were mostly taken up by floor-to-ceiling windows, one of which slid open to the balcony. It gave McNabb an excellent panoramic view of Manchester, the dense congregation of diverse buildings that created a playground for him and his business. He was particularly impressed by the Hilton Tower and how it rose much higher than the buildings around it. It was a feeling he understood.

Next to the front door was a flight of spiral stairs leading up to a balcony in which there was a small office. Why he needed an office at home was a mystery to most people, including McNabb himself. He did all his work at the Gold Force office or various cafes, bars and hotels when he was on the move. The apartment was his sanctuary, a place of relaxation and socialising.

That night, however, there was work to be done. He climbed the stairs and sat at his desk. It was bog standard, not like the grand oak table at headquarters, and McNabb realised that his PC was no longer the latest model. He booted it up and started planning.

It would be Edinburgh, naturally. The company did send people to other parts of the country, to one of the smaller megaliths that Nigel liked to claim he owned, but Vaughn and the other top brass would be involved in this one. McNabb decided it would be Dylan's team who would take part and it would be Dylan's time to shine. He had been badgering McNabb for weeks to run his own road trip; he really thought he had something to prove. Yes, Dylan could lead three of his team members, and the finale of his story would be a visit to the Devil's Altar.

It didn't take long for McNabb to fill the other slots for the trip. Christine could go. She didn't need to see the altar; she was happy in her position and didn't seem to have any managerial aspirations, so there was no need to show her the way of things.

Rick's name came to mind. Rick the enigma, Rick the man with the unimpressive sales record. Would this motivate him? What *would* motivate him? McNabb knew little of this employee. Rick came to work, made small bonuses and went home; he didn't seem enthusiastic about anything. He was always in a hurry to leave. Sometimes he went for drinks with his colleagues and on one occasion McNabb had joined them, much to the group's excitement. He took advantage of the night out to observe his people. Dylan and Greg dominated the conversation whilst others chipped in. Rick didn't contribute much and seemed to spend most of the time chatting with Christine, one of the few people he seemed to connect with.

For a split second he considered sending Rick to the altar. It would be interesting to hear what he made of it, and it would be amazing if it did inspire him. Despite not knowing Rick very well, McNabb liked him and wanted him to succeed. But if Rick knew the secrets and didn't want to play ball, the alternative wasn't something McNabb wanted to contemplate. He'd been sickened when Nathan had first told him about it.

After his own experience at the Devil's Altar, McNabb had been brought to The Light. Vaughn was there, having been initiated some years earlier, decked out in full robes. Like Nigel, he carried on wearing them all day, even in the pub. McNabb had laughed at them both. He didn't laugh so much when they showed him the dagger.

It led to a lengthy explanation from Nigel about the history of the Devil's Altar. McNabb was fascinated to hear about the Druids who'd lived among the ancient Celts, and how they were believed to have mystical powers. He was told how Nigel's grandfather had been one of them.

'The Neo-Druids established a secret organisation in the eighteenth century and we've managed to keep it a secret. Not like those bloody Freemasons! They advertise at museum open days.'

After another round of drinks, Nigel explained that his grandfather had helped set up the National Grid in 1901 and his connections to the Druids had allowed him to utilise the altar. They ensured the privacy of the area by spreading rumours among the locals that it was haunted by witches. It had all run so smoothly for them.

'There's no need for expensive turbines,' Nigel had explained. 'The energy can be pumped from the stones straight to the National Grid and – hey presto – you can put the kettle on for a lovely cup of English tea.'

McNabb found his head beginning to hurt as Nigel delved further into descriptions of magnetic Earth currents and his genealogical connections to the ancient Druids. 'You look confused. Alan, get him another pint.'

It was all connected: Nigel's family, the National Grid, his place on the board of N-Ergise, and it had all made him filthy rich. McNabb wanted to wallow in the filth too, even if he did have some reservations about the dagger.

'Don't worry, it hasn't been used. It's mostly ceremonial,' Vaughn reassured him.

'What do you mean *mostly*?'

'Until you need to stab someone,' Alan added helpfully.

They told McNabb that they hadn't really stabbed anyone, at least not intentionally. Nigel had apparently once jabbed himself accidentally whilst trying to sheath it.

And that tradition of not intentionally stabbing anyone had been kept up. Every five years a promising salesperson had been sent on a road trip and they had all made it back. They were sold the success of the Mercury Group and had kept quiet about what they had seen. Vaughn hadn't even mentioned his own initiation to McNabb, despite them being thick as thieves.

McNabb knew Dylan would love it, too. As for Rick, he'd be sent to Scotland as a last roll of the dice. If it went badly, he'd probably just quit in frustration. He didn't appear interested in the business, so on his return to Manchester he could hand in his notice and prepare for an exit interview. He would be given a sparkling reference and a few phone numbers for people who could use a hardworking chap like him in their business. McNabb hoped that Rick would realise his own potential; he'd always suspected that Rick had low self-esteem.

There was also the matter of the last team member to send. McNabb was recruiting later that week and decided to send whoever they took on. He'd intended that the rookie join Dylan's team anyway, and a road trip would be an exciting start.

After an hour of preparing the paperwork, he decided to retire to bed.

Twenty-four

Alan waited a few seconds, expecting McNabb to talk. 'Everything okay there, Daniel?'

'Yes. Fine. So, Rick went to see the stones then?' McNabb said slowly.

'That's right. He turned up out of the blue at The Light. Wasn't that the plan?'

'The plan was for Dylan to go to the stones. We've had a few issues with Rick. The whole thing is cancelled. You can't take Rick to the stones!' McNabb's heart skipped so many beats that he grabbed the side of the pump to steady himself.

'Don't tell *me* about it. It's Nigel and Nathan who are running things, not you and me.' Alan sounded desperate to hang up.

'Alan, listen carefully to me. You've got to go...'

'I've got things to do. Bye...' And Alan was gone.

Shit! This wasn't right, it shouldn't have happened. McNabb shoved his phone back in his pocket and ran to the shop. 'Come on, we're going,' he said forcefully to the team, who had now formed a queue at the till. They didn't question him; instead, they abandoned their items and hurried back to the Range Rover.

McNabb quickly paid for the fuel and they were soon speeding along the road. The journey was silent. Nobody wanted to ask McNabb what was wrong and he had switched off the radio so he could think. This time Christine didn't try to hijack it.

Twenty-five

By the time he reached the far side of the copse, Rick still hadn't decided where to go. He ran towards a small path but soon ditched that idea and veered off to one side of it and down the hill. He kept on going until he came to a small dry-stone wall. Clambering onto it gave him a good view of the route he'd taken. Vaughn was at the front of the group, moving rapidly. His military fitness training was clearly still paying off.

As Rick slithered over the other side of the wall, he felt one trouser leg rip and his skin tear on one of the pointier pieces of masonry. Hitting the ground, he decided it was safer to keep low and near to the wall to avoid being spotted. He came to a corner that veered sharply left. Deciding he could risk getting off his hands and knees, he rose to his haunches and did a sort of quick waddle, like a penguin that was in desperate need of a shit.

Vaughn reached the point where Rick had gracelessly fallen over the wall, looked around and assumed that Rick had carried straight on. On the other side of the wall there was another path that twisted down the contour of a hill and out of view.

Vaughn vaulted the wall and sprinted down the path just as a red-faced and panting Paul arrived. Tessa was right behind him and they both climbed the wall and followed Vaughn down the path.

Rick heard their grunts and the squelching of their shoes in the wet grass fade into the distance. He could also hear an elderly wheeze that signalled Nigel's approach to the wall. Nigel stopped when he reached it and leaned against it. Good old dry stone walls; an obese elephant could climb them and they wouldn't topple.

Rick stopped moving and dropped to his knees so he could hear better and because he was knackered. Nigel's breathing was heavy but punctuated with laughter. Rick was still very confused by the mess he was in and this creepy villain's laugh wasn't helping.

Nigel slowly clambered onto the wall and sat down with his legs dangling over the opposite side. 'Let's not drag this out, young man,' he called out gaily.

Rick continued to creep along his chosen route. He didn't think his pursuer would be able to hear him, but all the same he kept it slow and quiet.

'I know you're still here. I had a great view of the wall after you fell off it. You never moved away from it,' Nigel shouted, turning his slowness at running into his greatest strength.

Rick briefly considered attacking him. Nigel was

an older man and, although Rick was physically unfit, he thought he could probably overpower him. But Nigel had the knife. Even if Rick successfully disarmed him, what then? He had no intention of using the knife on Nigel, and he was still lost and on the run; Injuring or immobilising his pursuer wouldn't ultimately help him.

Nigel slid off the wall, his feet sinking slightly into the boggy ground as he landed.

Rick raised his head and upper body to see if he could find an escape route. The wall came to an end at a wire fence and he stopped a few metres away. What now?

He could hear the sound of Nigel's feet squelching through the sodden grass about fifty metres away and closing in. There was only one thing for it: Rick was going to have to try and outrun an old man. He rose slightly, placed his hands on the muddy grass and lifted his bum to adopt the position of an Olympic sprinter. Three, two, one ... go! Rick pushed off with his hands and legs and ran straight forward.

Nigel heard him and turned, shocked to see this futile attempt at escape. At first he did nothing, then he realised that Rick was moving faster than he had during the previous chase. Nigel hurried after him, though he struggled to keep up. 'There's nowhere for you to go, you fool,' he panted.

Rick didn't care; he just wanted to put more

distance between himself and the oddball. The ground in front was even for about eighty metres, but then came the dreaded incline. Damn these Scottish hills.

The muscles in his legs were screaming in pain; they hadn't been worked so hard since he had played badminton as a teenager. He was gasping for breath yet he kept going, barely noticing his shin which still stung from his fall. He ran full pelt up the hill. His shirt stank like a raver's armpit at 2am.

Slowing briefly, he glanced back and saw that Nigel was a fair distance behind him. He turned and, to his utmost surprise, managed to build up his speed again. For a moment he forgot the danger he was in and felt oddly elated. *I've got to get into running properly. If I get home alive.*

At the brow of the hill, Rick turned to gaze back down. He could see the stone circle far off to his right, and Vaughn's mansion straight in front of him but further away. And coming up the hill Rick could see a geriatric with a long black coat tripping up and then scrambling to his feet. All the fight and all the chase were gone. Rick turned away and trotted down the other side of the hill, satisfied that he had given Nigel the slip.

He carried on jogging for about ten minutes. He passed through more fields, some of them home to those incredibly hairy yaks he'd seen on tourist posters. At one point he found himself in a minefield of cowpats and it took all his limited agility to avoid treading on one. When he was truly shattered he slowed down to walking pace, yet he didn't feel like stopping. He'd pulled off an escape, an actual escape from danger and probable death. How many other people could say they'd done that?

In the distance Rick could see the sun had almost completely set and he really didn't want to spend the night outdoors. He could just about make out the grey streak of a road about two miles in the distance. It seemed an obvious landmark to head towards.

It took half an hour to reach the road because the ground was boggy. As it was a proper road this time, Rick felt a massive sense of relief. He didn't have a clue which way to go, but guessed it would be best to head away from Vaughn's house.

Before long it was completely dark and Rick had only the three-quarter moon to see by. Looking into the sky, he saw millions of stars and paused for a second to take them in. *This is something you don't see every night in Manchester*, he reflected, *or indeed any night*. It was quite beautiful and he wished he'd seen them in better circumstances and maybe with company.

After trudging for half an hour, Rick saw the unmistakeable orange glow of a town or city on the horizon. He perked up and started to walk more quickly, knowing he could get help and that his ordeal would soon be over.

A road sign pointed out that he was one-and-a half-miles away from a town whose name he didn't recognise. He had to decide where to go first. He felt too tired to spend the rest of the night looking for the local police station, besides which it was probably one of those small towns where the police don't work after 7pm or on Sundays. He considered going to a local shop to see if they would let him use their phone, his own having run out of battery charge. No, there was only one place he wanted to be; he would feel a greater sense of safety in the local pub. It was the natural place to go at such an hour, and he still had just enough money for one pint.

The road led into a housing estate on the outskirts of the town. A sign with large lettering, styled as if a child had handwritten it, welcomed careful drivers. Rick wondered whether it would welcome dishevelled salesmen fleeing sinister conglomerates of murderous business leaders. He doubted it.

After passing rows of detached houses with immaculate gardens, Rick came to a high street. The usual suspects were all present and correct: hairdressers, dry cleaners, fish-and chip-shop, shoe repair and key cutters. They looked a lot more upmarket than the ones he'd seen in the Edinburgh housing estate, but most of them were closed. Only a small corner shop had its lights on.

Rick walked past the row of shops and crossed the road at the pedestrian crossing, despite there being no traffic. On the other side he followed the street a few metres to a crossroads. He stopped and looked down the other three roads. The one to his right led to a busy car park and he decided to head that way to see where everyone was going. It had to be either a restaurant or a pub.

It was a pub. Dragging his feet in exhaustion, Rick let out a huge sigh of relief and walked up the crazy-paved path leading to the entrance. There was no swinging sign, just large brass lettering over the door that read The Cock. *A bit unoriginal*, Rick thought. *But who cares? I can relax a bit now.*

It sounded rowdy inside and, as Rick pushed open the door, the noise that hit him felt unusually unpleasant. The main bar was populated by about thirty people. As Rick entered, four men near the entrance started to laugh. Others heard them and turned to stare, then several more joined in with the mirth, looking either amused or embarrassed at the sight of Rick.

Despite his suit having been laundered only a few hours earlier, he had already managed to tear his trousers and large patches of mud were splattered all over them and his anorak. He dreaded to imagine what his sweaty face looked like. Humiliated, he spotted an empty table and decided to nab it. He could still hear people's muttered comments as he rushed over to grab a chair. There were also some less-muttered ones.

'Anyone missing a scarecrow?' one man shouted from the other side of the room.

Rick sat down and buried his head in a menu, despite not intending to order food. He had entered The Cock in more or less the same way he had gone into The Light, but there he had felt welcome despite his oddness. This place wasn't friendly or welcoming; his boozy peers were not his comrades.

Once the atmosphere had returned to normal, Rick slipped out to the toilets and repeated his pub cleansing ritual. He filled the sink with hot water and as much liquid soap as he could squeeze out of the almost empty dispenser. Yet again he couldn't get rid of all the brown stains on his suit, but he did manage to clean his face and the cut on his leg. He cursed himself for leaving his bag of supplies at Vaughn's house. Without a plaster, he feared the cut would heal with the material from the trousers sticking to it.

When he returned to his seat, Rick knew he had to plan his next move. Despite being surrounding by people not involved with the Mercury Group, he really didn't feel like explaining himself to anyone. It wasn't that he didn't trust them, he just didn't know where to start. Maybe at the part where he nearly got killed, then he could work back? Would they believe the story better if it were put into context? There were parts of it that still didn't make sense to Rick, let alone someone out for a drink after work.

Where was Vaughn's house and the stone circle? He didn't recall any specific details, although he remembered Vaughn had said he wanted to show him how to succeed. The visit to the Devil's Altar was planned and the other heads of the company had been invited specially for it.

Rick tried in vain to work out exactly how it had all happened. What if he'd not done a runner from Edinburgh? Or what if he had decided to head south, or go straight back home and not bother with his little excursion? There were too many weird coincidences going on, and Rick doubted anyone would take him seriously. He was also seriously lacking in actual evidence of what had happened; he didn't think the police would believe him rather than four top business executives. It was too baffling.

Time for a drink, he decided. With the last of his change, he bought a pint of lager and returned to his chair. By now the other customers seemed used to his presence and his appearance didn't garner so many moronic sniggers. He sipped his drink slowly, still trying to think of a plan, but he just couldn't. It seemed like he was in the most ridiculous situation imaginable and he could see no way out. He was out of money and he was annoyed at himself for only buying a single train ticket, though he knew he'd never find his way back to the station in that isolated village.

After sitting with his own thoughts for about a quarter of an hour, he felt a sudden chill as the door opened behind him and a gust of wind blew in. He felt a different chill when he heard the voice of the man who had entered. 'Evening all. Lovely night for a flagon of ale.'

Rick spun round in his chair to see Nigel standing by the entrance with his arms raised. He looked like a quiz-show host who was expecting a reply to a catchphrase. The greeting he received was similar to Rick's: the cloak and old-fashioned dialect got a few laughs.

'They're all out tonight!' cried the man who had mocked Rick.

Rick quickly turned back, hoping he hadn't been spotted. He heard Nigel approach the bar and order a drink. *Oh God, what do I do? I can't make a scene, they'll all think I'm barmy.*

'Yoo-hoo! Rick, I'm over here,' Nigel called.

There was no point pretending he wasn't there. Rick turned and looked at his pursuer. Nigel was dripping in sweat but grinning, as if he were having a great night out. He turned casually to the barman and took his pint of ale before heading over Rick's table to sit opposite him.

As he flapped the long cloak to sit down, Rick saw the hilt of the dagger slipped into his belt. Surely Nigel couldn't possibly use it in here?

'You're a hard man to keep up with. I'm absolutely shattered,' Nigel panted cheerfully, his bushy moustache dripping with sweat.

'I thought I'd seen the back of you. Or at least the front of you before you tumbled down that hill.' Rick smiled falsely.

'A worthy adversary, I must say, but to the victor the spoils of war.' Nigel raised his glass to salute his own efforts.

'I suppose I should be impressed you found me.'

'Don't be. I've been romping around these parts for years, know this town well enough. The pub's one of the only places still open at this hour. Even the peelers knock off at six. No crime around here, you see.' Nigel winked and took a gulp of his drink. 'Nathan isn't the only one with property around here,' he added. 'I have a delightful hut not far from his house. The locals think I'm some sort of hermit.'

That explained the muddy trainers he was wearing when he arrived at the mansion. He must have walked there from his hovel.

'I don't see what you think you can do here,

in front of several members of the public,' Rick challenged.

'I'm not planning on doing anything in here. It's not the most inspiring place, not like The Light. Now that's an excellent pub, don't you agree?' Nigel paused, expecting an answer. He didn't get one. 'Oh, come on, you love that pub just as much as I do,' he said excitedly.

'Yes, okay. It is a great pub,' Rick admitted.

'That's the whole point of it. It's a gingerbread house to young binge drinkers, which is what most sales people are. Speaking of which, are you having another drink before we get on with things?' Nigel's left hand moved down to where the dagger lay beneath his cloak.

'I've heard of a last meal but never a last drink. But as you're offering, I'll have another pint.'

'I'll get it. You wait right here.' He jumped up and glided over to the bar.

What now? Is he actually thinking of using that thing on me? Rick looked around the room. He didn't feel he could run again. He remembered how much he'd had to drink, the wine and brandy earlier and then the lager; he was starting to feel sluggish.

Nigel returned with more drinks and a packet of crisps, which he opened along three sides and placed in the middle of the table in a sharing gesture. 'I hope Ready Salted are alright. They're usually a safe bet,' he said between mouthfuls of crisps.

'Are we just going to talk about trivial things for now? Is that how you people do it?' Rick picked up his pint glass but avoided the crisps.

'I don't know what you mean.' Nigel put on a pretty good act at sounding surprised.

'I mean is this how nutters do it? Talk you to death before actually killing you?' Rick asked.

'I'm sorry if I'm boring you. That certainly wasn't my intention,' Nigel replied apologetically.

'You're mad. You're tapped in the head.'

'No!' He banged his hand down on the table loudly. A few people looked up from what they were doing. 'I'm not mad, I'm just a little eccentric. There is a difference, you know.'

'Really? Well, just what *is* that difference?' Rick was starting to feel more annoyed than fearful.

'The difference is simple. Think what you've heard during the last few years at work. Think of the one thing all your colleagues are obsessed with. Can you tell what it is yet?'

Rick said nothing.

'Money, young man. It changes everything. If I didn't have any money and I acted as I do, then you'd be bang on. I would be as mad as a manufacturer of hats. But as it is, I'm rich and that means I'm eccentric!' Nigel's tone was triumphant.

Both men relaxed back into their chairs and continued drinking. Rick heard the front door open again but paid no attention to the figure that approached the bar – until he heard his voice. 'Get me a pint of Guinness, would you?' came an arrogant, thrusting tone.

Rick didn't know whether to start crying or burst into song. Standing only a few metres behind him was the man who had irked him so much from day one. Yet he couldn't feel too disappointed that he was there; he was effectively the only ally that Rick had.

Nigel didn't seem to recognise Dylan or react to his arrival. Rick wanted to turn around and make eye contact with his team leader, but didn't want to let on that he knew him. As much as Rick didn't want to admit it, Dylan showing up was his only chance of escape. Nigel wouldn't risk killing two people, would he? He couldn't cover that up.

'I don't fucking believe it!' Dylan exclaimed.

Nigel turned and, for the first time since Rick had met him, he looked confused.

'I might have known I'd find you in the pub.' Dylan was clearly addressing Rick, who had no choice but to turn in his chair and face his accuser.

Dylan paid for his drink and strolled over to the table. A few of the people who had seen both Rick's and Nigel's strange entrances had heard Dylan and now wanted to be an audience to this meeting.

'Daniel is not happy with you, Rick.' Without being invited, Dylan sat down on a spare stool at the table.

'Where is he?' Rick asked.

'Not far from here. We've been searching this area all evening for you,' Dylan turned to look at Nigel and it crossed Rick's mind that perhaps they hadn't met before.

'You must be one of the Gold Force lot,' Nigel said.

'Have you met Nigel from the Mercury Group, Dylan?' Rick was trying to think of a way to turn the situation to his advantage. He still didn't have any ideas.

'Nigel, hi! I've heard Daniel talk about you. I'm Dylan Carson, senior team leader at Gold Force.' Rick wasn't sure the word 'senior' was officially part of his title.

'Hello, Dylan. It's pleasure to meet you,' Nigel said fairly convincingly.

'I've got a lot of ideas I'd like to run by you, if you've got the time,' Dylan suggested eagerly.

'Maybe another day,' he replied.

'Yes, now is not a good time. We're leaving.' Rick put down his glass and pushed his chair back slightly.

'No, we're not, Rick. We're going to stay here. For now, anyway,' Nigel insisted.

'He's right. We should stay here a while. I bet Nigel and I have got so much we can talk about.' Dylan sounded giddy.

'Look, we are not staying here, Dylan! You're

going to drink up and then we're going to leave through that door.' As he spoke, Rick threw his arm across the table and gestured to the door. On the way, his hand smacked into Nigel's pint glass, sending it right into him. Three-quarters of a pint of locally-brewed ale spilled over Nigel's lap. He jumped back, receiving laughter and sarcastic applause from the few patrons who were still watching the trio.

'You clumsy twat! Here, Nigel, I'll get some napkins.' Dylan reached over to grab some from the next table.

'No, don't. It's okay, don't worry.' Nigel no longer wanted to be the joker and looked genuinely annoyed. 'I'm just going to the toilets. Don't let him leave,' he said to Dylan as he pointed at Rick.

'Don't worry, he isn't going anywhere.' Dylan shot an angry look at Rick.

Rick remained silent until Nigel was out of earshot. 'Where's Daniel?' He was desperate to find out that his hopes hadn't been raised unnecessarily.

'He's out looking for you. We've all been, ever since you cocked up my road trip.'

'Forget about the road trip for a second,' Rick pleaded. 'A lot of very weird things have happened and we're in danger.'

'Do you think I'm stupid?'

'Look, Dylan, I'm sorry if I screwed up your big opportunity, but you've got to listen to me. The

Mercury Group isn't as amazing as it seems.'

'I suspect you've always thought that,' Dylan interrupted.

'They showed me how they made themselves so successful. It's all about ancient stone circles and murder and something to do with the energy suppliers and ownership of them. I must admit, I didn't really understand that bit,.'

'That's insane. Have you lost it?'

'No, Dylan. Look at me, I look like shit! How do you think I ended up like this?'

'I don't know.' Dylan shrugged.

'I've been chased over the Scottish countryside for the last two days by these psychopaths!' Rick was nearly shouting.

'What psychopaths?' Dylan sounded confused, but not entirely disbelieving.

'Vaughn and Tessa and Patrick-fucking-Bateman over there.' He pointed to the toilets, looking over to make sure the man in question wasn't about to return.

'Okay, so the people on the top are a bit weird. But they're not mad. They're just eccentric.'

'They *are* mad. Please, Dylan, can we just go?' Rick begged.

Dylan shook his head.

Rick thought he'd try a different approach. 'What exactly did Daniel tell you all to do tonight?'

'He sent us off to different villages to look for you.

He's driving around looking for you too.'

This was interesting news. It didn't sound like Daniel was part of the plan. Maybe he wasn't in on it; after all, he wouldn't send a search party out if he was. He'd try to distance himself from the whole situation.

'What did he say you should do when you found me?' Rick asked.

'He said to take you back to him straight away,' Dylan admitted.

'Then why are we waiting here? We've got to get in touch with him now.' Rick glanced towards the toilets, knowing they didn't have much time left.

Dylan let out a long sigh. 'Ok we'll go then. Although I don't know when I'm going to get a chance to talk to someone as senior as Nigel again,' he moaned.

'Trust me, you're not missing out. Let's go.' Rick stood up.

The two salesmen went straight to the door. There were disappointed grumblings from the audience whose evening out had become so entertaining. After emerging from the pub, Rick led them down the road in the opposite direction he had come from. Dylan looked as though his command had been stolen from him.

'What's the plan then, Wavell?' he goaded.

'Get your phone out,' Rick demanded, ignoring the obscure reference.

'I don't think I've got any reception.' Dylan took out his mobile to confirm this was true.

'Shit! We need to find a phone box.'

'I think there was one over by the post office.' Dylan pointed to some buildings further along the road.

'Let's go, then.' Rick turned and hurried off with Dylan in pursuit. He went about fifty metres before Dylan called out that they needed to turn left. They moved down another avenue, occasionally glancing back to make sure that Nigel wasn't following.

After emerging from a small snicket at the end of one road, they saw the familiar yellow lettering on a red background that read POST OFFICE. The phone box in front of it was also an old-fashioned red one, the type that the council loved restoring for the sake of tradition.

'Have you got any change?' Rick enquired.

'Always.' Dylan hurried into the booth, desperate to take control. Rick stood guard outside. It was an antiquated way to call for help, but they had few other options.

'Daniel? Hi, it's Dylan.' Rick heard him say, then he made the near-fatal mistake of turning excitedly to hear what else his team leader would say.

'Yeah, I've found him. But something weird happened. Fuck!' Dylan pointed desperately past Rick with a panicked look on his face.

Rick spun round and saw a fuming Nigel hurtling towards them. His black robe was billowing behind him as though he were a dark wizard. The knife was drawn and he had a look in his eyes that Rick thought would haunt him forever.

Rick tried to move but he couldn't; panic had frozen him. Nigel, a few paces away, drew his hand back, ready to slash. Rick heard the door to the phone box open and felt a strong pair of hands shove him hard in the back. He fell to the floor as the blade flew where his head had previously been. The knife hit the wooden booth and stuck there hard.

Dylan yanked the phone's handset as hard as he could, dislodging it before leaping outside. He swung the broken handset straight at Nigel's head; it made an awful cracking sound and sent Nigel reeling. The old man grunted as he hit the cold paving slab.

Dylan jumped over his prostrate body, grabbed Rick by the arm to pull him upright, and they fled. They ran for about half a mile before they were both out of breath. They were at the opposite end of the town to the point where Rick had arrived.

'How much did you tell Daniel?' Rick realised that, in his scaredy-cat state, he had missed the end of the conversation.

'I told him where we were and I just had time to say that Nigel was trying to kill us before I committed criminal damage,' Dylan replied.

'Thanks for that.' Rick meant it.

'Okay, don't get all touchy-feely on me. Daniel should be coming to find us.'

'Brilliant! We have a way out.'

'Not if Nigel finds us first. I don't think he was unconscious.' Dylan seemed to be rather proud of his moment of action.

They moved off the pavement and found a dryish patch of grass to sit on behind a large hedge and out of sight of the road. The only problem was that they were out of sight of McNabb, should he arrive.

They didn't talk for several minutes. Rick thought Dylan looked satisfied with his first-ever assault. His adrenalin must have soared. As they waited, the occasional sound of cars passing caught their attention. Each time Dylan got up and peered around the side of the hedge. When he realised it wasn't Daniel, he withdrew his head. Any locals might have mistaken him for a Peeping Tom.

'Can't be long now,' he said hopefully. 'I wonder if we'll be going back to the Edinburgh office tomorrow morning.'

'You're not still thinking about the job, are you? Do you really want to be out selling tomorrow?' Rick moaned.

'What happened up here was a minor setback. I can still salvage this road trip.'

The conversation was interrupted by the faint

sound of footsteps at the end of the street. The two men froze, straining their ears, and the sound got nearer. Rick instinctively slid underneath the hedge. Dylan looked at him like he was mad. 'The pavement is on the other side. He's not going to see us here,' he whispered.

'I'd rather not take that chance. Come on, get under here,' Rick hissed.

'I'll get filthy.'

'I've spent the last two days getting covered in mud. You'll cope, believe me.'

Dylan relented and, feet first, crawled quietly into position next to Rick. Luckily, the nearest street lamp was several metres further down the road, so their four feet weren't visible at the base of the hedge.

Rick and Dylan held their breath as the sound of trainer-padded footsteps grew closer and then slowed. Nigel stopped a few paces away from the hedge, came level with their hiding place and paused. But then the footsteps continued. It was only when they were in the distance that Rick let out a sigh.

It was another five minutes before they heard the next car approaching. Dylan hurried out of the bush.

'What are you doing? It might not be him,' Rick said.

'It's Daniel, I know it. That's a Range Rover. You

can tell by the sound of the engine. Come on!'

They scampered out from underneath the hedge and ran onto the road. Dylan waved his arms above his head to flag the vehicle down. Rick could just see Daniel's face; it was the first time he'd seen him looking anxious.

As they jumped into the car, Rick couldn't be sure but he thought he heard Dylan say 'shotgun' before flinging open the front passenger door and jumping in. Rick got in the back. He was surprised that he didn't feel the vehicle going from nought to sixty in a few seconds. *Why are we still stationary?*

McNabb turned to look at Rick. 'Are you okay?'

'As much as I can be right now. We've got to go. Step on it!' Rick yelled, surprised by his own anger and even more surprised that McNabb did as he said. They sped off through the quiet streets and in a couple of minutes were back in the countryside. Nobody spoke.

Twenty–six

Christine stood outside a small Co-op in the tiny village where she'd been dumped by McNabb. She was stamping her feet and rubbing her arms to keep warm, still missing the hot climate of her childhood.

At first she'd thrown herself into her role as a rescuer with vigour, but it hadn't taken long to explore the village and she soon realised that Rick wasn't there. He wasn't likely to be hiding in any of the gardens – too near to other people. That left the few shops that were still open and the pub.

The Moorlands was small, in keeping with its location. It had a low roof which the tall locals had to watch out for to avoid smacking their heads every time they went to the bar. The pub had two rooms for patrons. In the tap room two men sat quietly chatting; the rest of the bar was just as quiet, with only a couple of bored-looking individuals nursing pints.

Christine ordered half a lager and tried to make it last an hour. After about forty minutes, she became frustrated and got up to leave. 'See you later, love,' the barman called out. *Unlikely, she thought.*

194

Despite the cold, she thought she'd wait where she'd been dropped off. McNabb had told her he'd meet her there later, a lack of specifics that didn't inspire much confidence. She took out her phone and waved her arm around to see if she could catch a bit of precious signal. Looking at the screen, she realised that no one had tried to contact her.

Outside the Co-op was a large rock which Christine used as a seat. A passer-by stopped beside her. Christine reluctantly looked up at him, for once not wanting to talk.

'You know you're sitting on two hundred years of dog wee?' he said, laughing.

Christine looked back at him blankly.

'Dog walkers always come here. The dogs use that rock.' He pointed between her legs.

'It doesn't matter, I'm fine,' she said, managing to force a smile.

'Suit yourself.' He shrugged and went on his way.

Christine wondered if Jamie was having as bad a time as she was. She wanted to be back with the team but they were all miles away. She cursed Rick; he had dragged them across the country for no good reason. Why hadn't he just quit when they were back in Manchester? They could have kept in touch, met up for a coffee or a pint. Why did he have to be so awkward? And after everything she'd told him.

She heard the faint sound of Blondie's 'Atomic'

coming from inside her pocket. She fumbled out her phone. It had one bar of reception and the caller ID read *Dylan Work*. She answered. 'Hi Dylan. What's going on?'

'We've found Bear Grylls,' Dylan joked, not realising that Christine didn't know where Rick had been.

'What?' She sounded annoyed.

'Rick. I found him and we're with Daniel now. We'll meet you at the Co-op in ten minutes.'

'Okay, see you then.' She hung up before Dylan could reply. Finally, it was over. What would occur next, Christine could only guess. Would they go back to Edinburgh, or would the disaster that kept on giving come to an end? She just wanted to get back home for a hot bath and a long period on the sofa in her pyjamas.

She got up and started pacing around to keep her blood circulating. Every so often she looked at her watch, despite knowing that the ten minutes couldn't possibly be up. After fifteen minutes the Range Rover sped onto the village's main road and pulled up in front of her. She ran around to the far side and took a seat next to Rick.

Twenty-seven

It wasn't long before they found Jamie. He'd been given his own tiny village for his part of the quest to find Rick, and they found him sitting on a crumbling wall next to an abandoned cottage. He was in a world of his own and didn't notice the sudden presence of the large Range Rover, even when it pulled up right in front of him. McNabb honked the horn, almost causing to Jamie to tumble over the other side of the wall. He got in, without saying anything.

Uncharacteristically, Rick broke the silence. 'Where are we going now?' He leaned forward towards McNabb.

'I'm getting all of you the hell out of this country. In a few hours we'll be back in Manchester,' he said, keeping his eyes on the road.

'What about Maximus?' Dylan said.

'Who?'

'My car. It's still in Edinburgh.'

McNabb groaned. 'Okay, so it might take a bit longer.'

Despite being packed in the back with Christine and Jamie, Rick managed to fall asleep. He drifted in and out of slumber, occasionally hearing the sound of Christine snoring. Finally he felt the vehicle slowing down and woke up to see that they were turning off the road.

They pulled up at a small petrol station. 'Let's get some food,' McNabb said unenthusiastically.

They got out and stretched before heading to the shop. Inside it was almost empty, apart from one man mopping the floor and the cashier who looked like she really wanted to be somewhere else – judging by the fashion magazine her nose was stuck in, probably Milan. By the till there was a coffee machine and a glass cabinet containing bacon and sausage sandwiches. McNabb grabbed a few of them and went to pay.

They stood around the vehicle eating in silence. Rick looked at McNabb, expecting him to say something, anything, about what had happened – some sort of explanation. McNabb looked back at him and said nothing.

'I think we need to talk about what happened,' Rick ventured as they finished eating.

'Don't worry, I'll explain everything to you,' McNabb said.

'Well, now's as good a time as any. I think you owe me.' Rick didn't know where this sudden aggression came from.

McNabb looked taken aback by it too. 'I promise I will tell you everything, just not whilst we're standing in a car park at the side of the dual carriageway.' His voice dropped so only Rick could hear. 'And not in front of these.' He flicked his head to indicate the rest of the group.

'You'll have to tell them something eventually.'

'Let me worry about that,' he hissed.

Rick decided to leave it. He didn't want to start an argument at this point. He would wait; he would give McNabb time to think up a good explanation and he'd listen patiently to it.

He considered how much McNabb had to lose. Even if he wasn't involved in the Mercury Group's more violent side, he was still aware of it. Rick didn't know enough about the law to know if McNabb would be liable for what happened or not, but even if he wasn't charged his reputation would still be ruined. He could lose Gold Force and any other small businesses he had invested in. Rick couldn't decide if he should feel sorry for him or not – but McNabb had sent him on a road trip that had nearly got him killed.

'Are we all finished now?' McNabb asked the group, who were draining coffee cups and wiping ketchup off their fingers.

'Where are we going?' Christine asked without her usual whimsy.

'Once we've picked up Dylan's car, it's up to you lot. I can carry on driving south all night and have us back in Manchester by the wee hours of tomorrow morning. It won't be a comfortable ride, but we can do it. Alternatively, we can stay in a hotel somewhere in the north of England.' McNabb presented the options without hinting which one they should go for.

'I'm too tired to pull an all-nighter, especially if I'm driving,' was Dylan's response.

'I think the hotel would be the best idea,' Jamie added.

'Yes, we should get a good night's rest,' Christine agreed.

'Ok, hotel it is.' McNabb shrugged. It seemed odd to him getting such an unimpressed, pragmatic response to his suggestion. Usually, his employees would sell their granddad's left testicle for such an opportunity.

They piled back into the Range Rover and tried to get comfortable. It was easier for Dylan, who still insisted on being in the front. McNabb pressed a switch on the dashboard which elevated a small TV screen, like something Q-Branch might provide. Below it was an equally small keyboard into which he skilfully tapped a few words. The screen came up with a list of hotels in the North West. McNabb chose the third one down. 'Oh yes, this one is excellent,' he said.

Why can't he just go for the nearest? Rick was annoyed that, even in a situation like the one they were, in his rich boss was being picky about where they stayed.

A couple of hours, several broken snoozes and one massive awkward silence later, the vehicle slowed. Rick jolted upright when he realised that he recognised the large expensive houses around him. They pulled up outside Vaughn's house.

'Okay, Dylan, are you happy to follow me?' McNabb had evidently discussed the convoy back home whilst the others had slept. Dylan nodded and got out. He ran over to his car and jumped in, waiting for McNabb to move off.

'The front's free,' McNabb hinted, but nobody could be bothered moving. 'Come on, this isn't a taxi.' He sounded amused, but Rick suspected that it would actually bother him to look like a taxi driver, even in an expensive car. He decided to humour his boss and got into the front passenger seat.

As soon as McNabb set off, Dylan was right behind him. For the first ten minutes of the journey McNabb kept checking the rear-view mirror to ensure he was still there. In the early hours they exited the M6 and soon after entered an historic-looking town. It was Penrith.

Rick had been there for a weekend a few years previously and had enjoyed the laid-back environment; he wished he felt as relaxed on his current visit. The town didn't seem as welcoming when you were escaping across the border from certain death. He was starting to feel like a cowardly Communist defector heading to West Berlin.

They drove into the town centre and passed the clock tower, which was impressively illuminated. A few minutes later they approached a hotel. It certainly looked like the type of place a Mercury Group MD would stay in; it was a large Victorian building with a grand entrance flanked by stone lions on either side of the double doors. It looked quite busy, with lights on in many of the rooms.

McNabb drove past the entrance to the turning that led to the busy car park. Rick suspected that the hotel had a restaurant and bar that were used by non-guests. Despite the unusual situation in which the team found themselves, Christine and Jamie still looked up at the building in awe. This was the type of place they had been promised they would stay in on business trips if they progressed, this and first-class flights and valet service.

Rick's suitcase had been brought from Vaughn's house and was in the large boot. He was glad to have some possessions again, having left his small bag at Vaughn's Edinburgh house.

They filed into the lobby and found the interior just as exquisite as the outside. There was a large staircase that wouldn't have looked out of place on the *Titanic*. It rose up and stretched round both sides of the large hall. From the high ceiling dangled large chandeliers with old-fashioned lamps attached to each arm. The furniture was plush and there were several red wing-back chairs with important-looking men in designer suits lounging on them with glasses of brandy.

Rick felt like walking over to one of them and punching him in his rich smug face – he'd had enough of those types. He had to content himself by merely glaring at them. They seemed not to care.

The concierge looked excited by McNabb's arrival and a little confused by the party of slightly dirty or, in Rick's case very dirty, people he had arrived with. 'Lovely to see you again, sir.' He shook McNabb's hand.

'The same to you, Karl. I wonder if I could have my usual room and four others for my colleagues.'

'Yes, of course, I'll get straight on it. If you could just give your names to Maggie, please.' Karl turned to the receptionist.

One by one the team walked up to the desk and gave Maggie their names and addresses. The concierge dished out the keys, which weren't actual keys but swipe cards, and directed them to their rooms. Rick was pleased that his was in a separate wing of the building. He bade everyone good night before traipsing up the stairs to find room eighteen.

As expected after another long journey, Rick was tired. He had half a mind to get into bed with his clothes on, but the white-linen sheets on the vast king-sized bed looked too nice to ruin and he opted instead to run a bath. The en-suite's size reminded Rick of the vast bathroom at Vaughn's manor. Every metal surface had been highly polished and the accessories looked brand new.

Rick half-filled the bath and soaked for ten minutes before he decided he'd fall asleep and drown if he remained there much longer. He dried himself and found that his suitcase had been left in his room whilst he was in the bathroom. He hadn't heard a thing; it was as if a room-elf had slipped in and out, leaving it next to the bed for him.

Despite his previous lethargy, Rick no longer felt like sleeping. He opened his suitcase and pulled out a pair of jeans and a T-shirt. They were the only casual clothes he had brought for the trip.

He left his room and decided to find the bar. He knew he couldn't afford a drink but he wanted somewhere relaxing to sit whilst the many thoughts colliding in his head calmed down.

The hotel's bar was on the ground floor and didn't look like it was due to close, despite it being way after midnight. The bar was stocked with every kind of spirit imaginable and there were several pumps for lagers, ales and ciders. The solitary barman looked up enthusiastically at Rick's arrival but appeared slightly disappointed when Rick went straight to a table in the opposite corner and sat down without ordering a drink.

The room was large and full of circular tables surrounded by stools, apart from an empty space in the corner which was used as a dance floor should the room be hired out for functions.

Rick sat for several minutes, deep in thought about the week he'd had, until he sensed someone approaching his table. Christine took a seat opposite him and placed a glass of Coke down in front of her. Rick didn't know if he wanted company right then.

She didn't look very happy and seemed to be more tired than Rick. 'This was a fucking disaster,' she spat.

Rick assumed she meant the whole trip. 'I'm sorry about all this, Christine. I know you were looking forward to the trip. And I know my...' He looked for the right word.

'Selfishness?' Christine suggested.

'Yes. That ruined it. I should have just gritted my teeth and got on with it. It was only a week.'

Christine shook her head. Rick was surprised she was disagreeing with him. 'No, you shouldn't, because you shouldn't have come along in the first place. You obviously haven't been happy at work.'

A slight understatement. Rick didn't say it out loud.

'You should have said something earlier. Why didn't you tell Daniel? Why didn't you tell me, for God's sake?' She started to choke up. Although Rick had seen her break away from her usual joviality before, it still made him feel uneasy.

'The truth is, I'm a coward. I couldn't admit that I hadn't been happy to anyone. I can barely admit it to myself.'

'Do you think being self-deprecating makes it all okay?'

'No, but I really can't think of anything else to say right now.'

'I opened up to you that time. I told you everything.'

Rick was about to try and explain that he hadn't avoided speaking to her on purpose, but Christine carried on. 'You could have spoken to me loads of times, but you didn't.' She started to sob quietly. Rick pushed back his stool to get up and sit next to her, but he was too slow. She jumped up and near enough ran out of the bar.

Rick stayed in his seat. It was all true; Christine had once spent a whole evening pouring her heart out to him. It was after work and they'd gone back to Christine's flat. She said that she'd been back on the meds and at first Rick was confused; Christine seemed like the last person who would need medication for her moods.

She told him about losing a close friend when she was in her teens. She hadn't dealt with it well and, combined with the usual problems of any child at that age, she'd been diagnosed with depression.

It didn't affect her all the time and she could go through long periods without it, but occasionally she hit what a doctor had once called a 'downward spiral'. She hated the expression because it sounded too clichéd, but she also lived in fear of it happening again. She normally surrounded herself with sympathetic people, but had once told Rick that all the love and support from her friends and family couldn't alleviate the feeling of shittiness she felt at the worst times.

Rick cursed himself bitterly for not trusting Christine like she had him. He suspected she hadn't brought her meds on the road trip. She'd expected to have an excellent time.

Rick didn't stay long in the bar. He slumped off back to his room and climbed into bed.

Twenty-eight

A loud banging noise awoke Rick from a deep sleep. It took a few moments for him to remember where he was and why he was in such a luxurious room. *Ah yes, I'm travelling with a rich man.* He cringed with embarrassment and regret at the last thing that had happened before he went to bed.

'Rick, get dressed. Daniel doesn't want to hang around here too long.' Dylan's slightly raised voice came through the door.

'I'll get up now,' Rick called back.

'Right, I'll see you in the breakfast lounge in a minute,' Dylan said before Rick heard his footsteps fading away. *The breakfast lounge? Do they have a different room for each meal?*

Rick showered and dressed in his work gear. He was grateful to have a clean shirt and trousers as well as a fresh pair of socks and underpants. He only had the one blazer and would have to make do with that.

The hotel seemed busy at 9.30am. As Rick made his way to the breakfast lounge, he passed several tourists and a number of folk he assumed were on business trips. He wondered if theirs had been as eventful as his.

Rick was confronted by a rather impressive display of foods, everything you could possibly want before 11.30 in the morning. A long table stretched across one side of the large room; at one end was a selection of cereals, fruit juices and the hot beverage machine. There was the usual array of breakfast dishes, as well as those that not many people really like but are sometimes there anyway such as black pudding and mushrooms so big that a Smurf could perch on them. There were yoghurts, both English and American muffins, pancakes, fruit, toast, croissants, Danish pastries and waffles.

Rick spotted a table occupied by McNabb, Dylan and Jamie. He assumed Christine was still getting ready and was relieved she wasn't there. As soon as he sat down, he was up again without a word to the team and making his way towards the buffet. He filled a plate, grabbed some coffee and beat a hasty retreat to the table.

'You must be hungry,' McNabb said trying to sound as at ease.

Rick murmured an agreement. Dylan and Jamie were part way through their breakfast but McNabb didn't have a plate before him, just a mug of black coffee.

After Rick finished, he leaned back. 'So, what happens now?'

'Daniel wants to be out by ten thirty,' Dylan said before Daniel could open his mouth.

'That doesn't give us a lot of time,' Rick said.

'Time for what?' McNabb asked, knowing full well what Rick meant.

'A much-needed explanation,' Rick replied.

All eyes were on McNabb, waiting for a response, for an opinion. He sighed and made up his mind. 'Rick's right, I do owe you all an explanation. Especially you.' He looked at Rick. 'Which is why I'm going to knock our timings back a bit. We'll leave here at eleven. Dylan, Jamie, if you two could occupy yourselves until then – I'm sure you'll understand that I really need to explain things to Rick first.' They both nodded and got up to leave.

Rick watched them go. Christine still hadn't appeared and he hoped she wouldn't come down during his conversation with McNabb. He wouldn't be able to stand seeing another disappointed look on her face as she was sent away.

'I think we should find somewhere a little more private,' McNabb suggested.

'Fine by me.' Rick pushed back his chair and waited for his boss to get up and lead the way. They went through the reception area and down a corridor that led to another part of the hotel. Further along the corridor was a lounge. As they entered, Rick was disappointed to see there were at least six people in there, minding their own business, reading the broadsheets.

'Through there.' McNabb pointed towards a set of French windows that led onto a wooden veranda. It was empty. He closed the windows behind them and indicated a seat for Rick. He took his own seat and for about a minute they sat in silence, looking onto the vast lawn where a group of children were playing with a frisbee. Rick felt a pang of jealousy. Their life was simple; they hadn't endured anything as weird or as unsettling as he had.

As McNabb wasn't saying anything, Rick decided to start the show. 'This might seem like an obvious question,' he began. 'But why?'

'I don't suppose any answer I give will be completely satisfactory. And I don't just mean to you, I mean to the police as well,' McNabb murmured.

'Yes, I did wonder how you were going to explain it to them,' Rick considered.

'As long as I've been in my position, nobody has ever been hurt during an initiation. Sometimes I'd hear of other managers' choices and it would worry me if it was someone I was unsure of, someone who didn't seem like they'd quite taken to it.'

'Like me.' Rick slumped back in his seat and cast his eyes across the game in front of him.

'It happens every five years. Someone is picked from one of the Mercury Group's offices. Dylan was the natural choice when it came to our turn, although I did consider you for a second. Christine and Jamie completed the team but I would never have sent them to the altar, especially not Jamie.'

'I'd really hate to imagine how he'd have taken it.' A shiver ran down Rick's spine as he imagined the scared young man being chased across a moor by Nigel, his cloak flapping like a vulture's wings as he waved the dagger about.

'I really did send you there to succeed, Rick. You weren't just there to make up the numbers. I have a lot of respect for you and I thought it would help improve your performance.'

Rick wasn't interested in praise. 'Fair enough, but what's the rest of the story?'

'It was all nicely set up. I'd been dropping hints about The Light to Dylan for weeks. The leaflet in the kitchen at Vaughn's house was meant to be the final bait. All it would have taken was a phone call from me advising him exactly where to go. You know there's a much less muddy way of getting from Lochglen station to The Light?' McNabb ventured, attempting to get a laugh from Rick.

'Maybe one day you could take me back up there and show me around. We could reminisce about this trip,' Rick said slowly through gritted teeth.

'I'm sorry. I'm just so impressed you found it the way you did.' Before Rick could retort, McNabb hurried on. 'Anyway, Dylan was meant to meet Vaughn. I'm sure he'd have been disappointed to find that The Light wasn't a fully functioning modern conference suite.

'It was all fine until I got the call from Dylan saying you'd done a runner. I tried to call the team of directors but couldn't get through to anyone all afternoon. I decided to travel up to Edinburgh and deal with the situation personally. Eventually I got through to Vaughn and found out you were okay. By that point I was in Scotland and decided to carry on. The road trip was over as far as I was concerned, and Dylan would have to postpone his rise to glory. It just remained for me to reunite the team and bring you all back home.'

'Then what happened?' Rick urged.

'I called Nathan's mansion again and spoke to Alan. He told me you'd been taken to the altar. I was fuming – it wasn't supposed to happen. If I ever see Nathan again, I'll ask him why it did whilst I kick his head in.' McNabb turned away to look across the grass in an attempt to hide his anger.

'If you feared the worst, why did you send the team out looking for me? You must have thought I was dead,' Rick said in a less-traumatised voice than the statement warranted.

'When I drove to the mansion, I parked the Range Rover at the gate and told the team to wait for me. It was dark and I decided to approach on foot. I was being very stealthy, all black ops. Anyway, as I was nearing the entrance, I heard voices. I decided to hide behind a bush and listen, even though I didn't really need to.' McNabb knew this was a story he would have to tell again several times, so he appreciated the rehearsal.

Despite being sick to death of stories, Rick listened. It seemed like the blanks were finally being filled in.

'Paul, Tessa and Nathan were arguing as they approached the house. I heard Nathan angrily demand to know where Nigel was. Tessa guessed he was still looking for you. That seemed to rile Nathan even more and he said something along the lines of "that mad old git won't be able to catch him".'

'He wasn't wrong there.' Rick was still quite proud of his long sprint.

'I realised their plan had failed, and that you were out there somewhere being hunted down. I waited until they'd gone inside and went back to the Rover. I know that area reasonably well and dropped off the team in different villages. You know the rest of the story.'

'Yes. You found me and here we are. The question is what happens next?' Rick hoped for a decent answer.

'When we get back, I'll drop you home. I don't suppose you'll mind having a holiday for a few days. In the meantime, I'll go and talk to the Greater Manchester Police and tell them everything. Then everyone at Gold Force will have a holiday – until they can find new jobs.'

'Where do you think Vaughn and the rest of them are?' Rick asked.

'They'll have left the country. They don't know I tried to help you, so I could get in touch with them. I might even be able to help the police find them.'

'Did you know that Dylan hit Nigel with a payphone?'

'Did he?' McNabb said, surprised.

'Yes, when he called you yesterday. Nigel knows he works for you and has probably guessed we both went back to you. I doubt he'll be too keen to tell you which Caribbean island he's on.'

'Let me worry about that. You just enjoy your time off. I'll give you a bonus on payday. You've suffered enough for it.'

'Thanks. I could do with it,' Rick said, not entirely sarcastically.

'The ramifications of all this could be massive. Thousands will lose their jobs when N-Ergise folds.' McNabb groaned and put his hands up to his forehead.

'I never thought of that whilst I was running for my life. But yes, a lot of people probably will lose out. What's the deal with all that Druid stuff and the National Grid?'

'The deal?'

'You said that every five years a rep is taken there.

Are you trying to tell me that every single one of them believes that's how the whole country is powered?' Rick probed.

'Surely by now you've realised why no bugger questions it? They're being inducted into a very exclusive and successful group. It's an opportunity.'

'An opportunity to get rich,' Rick said, as if money were suddenly a deadly disease.

'Well, yes. If you're making large bonuses, you aren't going to give a toss if the boss is insane. Besides, there are plenty of naïve and superstitious people out there. I'm sure some of them believe in the supernatural,' McNabb pointed out.

'When you put it like that, it makes a lot of sense.'

'I've no idea what the police will say about the altar and Nigel the Druid. By the way, they'll be in touch with you soon so, you know, don't go abroad or anything,' he joked.

'Don't worry, I won't be going far.' Rick got up to leave.

Twenty-nine

It didn't take him long to pack his suitcase and go down to the lobby. He arrived fifteen minutes early and sank into one of the plush armchairs next to a rich old man. Maybe he could befriend him and get into his will.

It started to rain. As Rick watched the drops trickle down the window, he realised that if he hadn't been on the trip he would be facing a day trying to sell in the cold and wet. He wondered what would happen when he got back home. He wasn't sure if he should contact the police before they contacted him. He really didn't have the energy to describe his adventure just yet.

Jamie approached quietly and took a seat opposite Rick's potential Sugar Daddy.

'How are you, Jamie?' Rick asked.

'Okay, thanks,' he answered meekly.

Rick couldn't work out how bad the trip had been for him. He thought back to that night in Vaughn's Edinburgh house and the argument Jamie had with his dad. Just like Rick, Jamie clearly hadn't made much money but had the premature end to the whole expedition worried him? It was difficult to tell.

It was a good thing, Rick decided. Jamie might not appreciate it now – and Rick was certain Jamie's dad wouldn't – but when the company closed he'd be able to move on. Rick made a mental note to talk to him, maybe to warn him to keep away from sales jobs, maybe advise him to try university.

Over the next few minutes Daniel, Dylan and Christine arrived. Without speaking, the group took their bags and went to the car park. Christine didn't look as upset as she had done the night before, but she still avoided speaking to the others. They loaded up the two vehicles and took the same seats they'd been in when they arrived. It was McNabb's turn to switch on the radio; Rick suspected he did it to break the painful silence.

They were soon on the M6 heading south, with the edge of the Lake District on their right-hand side. McNabb put his foot down, not worried about a speeding fine. He didn't bother stopping for coffee and snacks; everyone just wanted to get straight back home.

Rick started to doze as they passed Lancaster. The deceleration was gradual, and it wasn't until they were on a 30mph road in the outskirts of Manchester that he woke up. It was a rather clandestine speed bump that jolted him back to life. He wasn't sure where he was, but a road sign informed him they were only three miles from the city centre.

'We won't go back to the office,' McNabb said.

'We're not going on another road trip, are we?' Christine asked sardonically.

'No, thankfully. I'm dropping you all home.'

Rick looked out of rear window and realised that Dylan was no longer following them. He seemed to remember that his former team leader lived somewhere in the Salford Quays.

The rest of the journey to Rick's flat didn't take long and all he could think about was how McNabb knew where they all lived, despite being away from the office and their files for almost two days. He could probably access them on his phone, or maybe he still used a Filofax. It didn't really matter; Rick was just glad to get home.

He wasn't sure how to leave the car. Would a simple 'bye' suffice? He went for it in the end, not that there was a very enthusiastic response.

Rick wondered if Callum would be in at this time. He walked slowly up the flight of stairs that led to the three flats on the first floor. There was no sound from any of them and Rick paused for a moment before inserting his key. He didn't know why, it wasn't as if he were trying to sneak up on his friend.

He entered the flat and removed his coat and shoes before heading to his bedroom to leave his suitcase. The main room was empty. Rick couldn't decide what to do. He was officially on holiday, but he didn't have that slightly excited feeling that a break from the norm usually brings, the feeling you first have as a child that never leaves you no matter how old you are. At the pub in Edinburgh Rick had thought of it as beating the system. Maybe that's what all holidays were, and you knew that even during the six-week holidays of childhood. No, that feeling seemed to have escaped Rick.

He decided to boil the kettle and relax for a couple of hours. When Callum returned, there would be a lot to explain. Rick considered texting him, but thought it would be more amusing to see the look on his face when he entered the flat and saw him there. Rick even considered bringing his swivel chair in from his bedroom to do a Blofeld-style reveal. *No, too much effort.*

After two cups of tea and an episode of *Bargain Hunt*, Rick decided that staying in the flat alone wasn't for him. He usually tried to get out and about during his occasional holidays. He'd visit friends in different parts of the country, or maybe go a little further afield if he could afford it.

He left the flat at around 3pm and wandered slowly down to the little corner shop. He remembered that he wouldn't have much money until payday at the end of the week. He wondered how much of a bonus McNabb would give him.

Rick walked past the shop and decided to head

for the local park instead. He spent the rest of the afternoon meandering around the trees and wondering how ducks would survive if kids didn't throw bread at them.

At around 5pm, he decided it was getting too cold and walked back to the flat. He didn't know when Callum would finish doing whatever it was he did during the day. *Maybe he works in the flat in secret when I'm not in. I hope he isn't a rent boy.*

Rick entered the flat but Callum wasn't there. He made a ham salad sandwich and sat in silence eating it. When he finished, he picked up a discarded copy of *The Mirror* that Callum had bought the previous day. Footsteps sounded in the corridor at around 6.30pm. Rick dropped the newspaper and jumped up to switch off the lights. *Might as well ramp up the dramatic effect.*

The door opened and Rick heard the thud of a rucksack being dropped before Callum bent down to remove his shoes. He came to the lounge door and switched on the light. 'Fuck me!' he exclaimed, jumping back slightly.

'Is that a request or a command?' Rick asked.

'It was an "I wasn't expecting you back so soon". What happened?'

'I've got a lot to tell you.'

'Where?' But he didn't need to ask.

o—● ●—o

It took a while for Callum to say anything. They were finishing their second pints by the time Rick got to the end of his story and Callum had been surprisingly quiet throughout. His continued silence frustrated Rick and he gestured impatiently with his hands. 'Well? What do you make of it?' he asked.

Callum paused with his glass part way to his mouth. He put on an exaggerated look of concentration before slowly placing it back on his beer mat. 'Just a couple of questions,' he stated.

'Go on,' Rick encouraged.

'How do ancient stone circles produce the type of energy that powers a Teasmade?' He didn't give Rick a chance to answer. 'And just one other, although it's quite an important one. Is any of your story true?' He sniggered.

'Yes, it's true! I'm not pissing around here! You've got to believe me, mate.' Rick put his very serious voice on.

'I'm sorry, but it all sounds a little extreme.'

'I know it's extreme. It was extreme when Nigel tried to kill me!'

'What's it like nearly being killed? In fact, don't answer that. I mean, you don't have to answer that if you don't want to,' Callum reassured a now very agitated Rick who, for the first time since Callum had known him, looked like he might punch him. 'This could only have happened to you. Probably because it's the type of thing that would never happen to you.'

They sat back and saw off the remainder of their pints, both attempting to work out the logic of that last comment.

Callum brightened again and leaned forward. 'You know what this means, don't you?' he said.

'What?' Rick could think of several things, but wanted to know what Callum had in mind.

'It means that after all these years of complaining about your job and not doing anything about it...' he paused for effect '...you've finally got what you want!'

Rick's response sounded pathetic. 'I don't feel like I've got what I want.'

'But you have! Alright, nearly being killed in the middle of nowhere wasn't great, but you'll get over that. What you couldn't get over was having to do the same job day in, day out and not feeling able to leave. You've escaped the company at last. You can do anything you want now and you're going to be paid a bit extra as well. McNabb might feel really guilty and pay out thousands.'

Rick had been hoping for a hefty pay out, and in the back of his head there had even been a bit of excitement and hope about what job he would do next. But it was always drowned out by the worry that jobs were hard to come by. 'You're right. In a weird way, I have got what I wanted. Does it always feel like this when that happens? It's not a brilliant feeling.'

'I think you're asking the wrong man. I'm nearly thirty and living in a flat with an unemployed man. I haven't exactly got what I wanted,' Callum said, not looking too disappointed.

Rick made a mental note to try and make the most of his situation and start a job hunt immediately. Or at least the next morning.

They didn't stay very late in The Earl. Rick was in bed by 11pm, where he slept like an exhausted log. In the morning he got up at 10am and lounged around the house, eating toast and job searching on the internet for a few hours. Finally he left the flat to look for work on the streets. The local corner shop still had a notice board for adverts, which Rick thought was a bit old fashioned, but he browsed it all the same.

Later in the week Rick went to his local police station and completed a witness statement. Describing his ordeal somehow didn't seem as strange as he'd thought it would. Like McNabb, the constable taking the statement advised Rick not to go away, although *he* didn't joke about it.

On the eve of Rick's return to work, he felt nervous. He didn't know how the office would react to him – after all, he had almost definitely caused the death of their workplace. Maybe they had heard about all the weirdness of the Mercury

Group and were glad to get out. He didn't know. He wanted to get in and out as quickly as he could.

o-• •-o

McNabb's night had been a little more turbulent because his penthouse sanctuary had been invaded by the forces of confusion and procrastination. He paced up and down, gesticulating to an imaginary audience, a thing he would have once derided in others. His tree had been well and truly shaken and he didn't like everything dropping out of it.

'What's wrong with me?' he almost shouted at his excellent view of the city, as if the free-standing structures would provide an answer.

Eventually he collapsed onto his sofa, embarrassed by his loss of self-control. Of course he knew what the solution to his problem was: he had to talk to the police, regardless of how much it incriminated him.

He remembered hearing that an old platoon sergeant of his from the 5th was now a detective sergeant in the Greater Manchester Police. He pulled out his phone and searched hopefully for the right name. Yes, it was there! With no further delay, he called the number.

'Hello,' a gruff Glaswegian voice answered.

'Dougie? It's Daniel McNabb here. How the hell are you?'

'Daniel, great to hear from you. Have you recovered since the reunion?'

'Only just. I've got something I need to discuss with you, face to face, if possible.' McNabb knew this would cost him a small fortune in real ale.

'No problem, what's it about?'

'It's a bit hard to explain.'

Thirty

The journey into the centre of town passed quickly. Rick was still nervous about the day ahead. *Am I really about to escape my hated job,* he asked himself. Yes, it seemed like that time had finally come. He knew he'd spend the next few weeks kicking himself repeatedly for not doing it sooner, but that day it didn't matter.

Manchester was as busy as usual. Over the tops of the buildings, he could see the Hilton Hotel and it reminded him of Scotland. He imagined for a second the downpour of glass that would await those below.

He entered the company building and, for the first time ever, he took the lift. He assumed that, as they were located on the second floor, most of his young, energetic colleagues would probably walk and this way he avoided bumping into anyone.

When he walked into the office, several heads turned his way. Greg, who was standing nearest, scowled as he walked by.

At least I know how they're going to react to me now. Rick decided to go straight to McNabb's office and take a seat outside. He passed Christine and Jamie on the way. Christine smiled sympathetically and he assumed he was forgiven.

Looking through the glass partition, Rick spotted McNabb working on his computer. Rick's bum had only been settled for about twenty seconds before the door opened and McNabb invited him in. Just before he entered, he turned back to look at the room and noticed he was attracting scornful glares. Rick spotted Dylan in conversation with one of the junior reps, trying to maintain his attention with some story or other. The rep, however, was more interested in the dickhead who was probably about to cut his job short and only reluctantly turned back to listen.

Rick entered the office and sat on the same chair he had done a couple of weeks previously. It seemed like a lifetime ago, a different time entirely. McNabb was sitting forward in his plush leather chair as if he meant business. Rick waited to hear what he had to say; he knew what was coming, but he couldn't guess how much of a build-up it would have.

'How was your break?' McNabb began.

'It was nice, thanks. Surprisingly relaxed, considering,' Rick answered.

'Good. I don't think we need to go through any of the formalities today, Rick. You didn't want a representative and, unless you've had a massive change of heart in the last few days, I'm assuming this is an exit interview.'

Massive change of heart or intense lobotomy, Rick thought.

'Yes, it is still an exit interview.'

'Normally HR would be here,' McNabb explained.

'Why aren't they?'

'Because I can't stand them.'

'Fair enough.' Rick didn't especially want any more people being added to this farewell.

'These interviews are usually conducted to find out why an employee wants to leave,' McNabb said with a glimmer of a smile, hoping Rick would see the funny side of that statement.

'I just didn't like the facilities.' He thought he'd play ball.

'I'll put a detailed explanation in later.' McNabb leant over his keyboard and bashed out a few words.

'Do you want me to go over any of the finer details?' Rick offered.

'No, I think you've given me the basics and they'll do. The various explanations from different people have given me enough to put the whole story together.'

'Really? There can't have been that much extra to get from Dylan and Christine.' Rick remembered the moment he'd hidden on the bus when he saw Jamie, and realised that Jamie knew even less.

'Oh, I got quite a lot of useful information from a

certain landlord.' McNabb smiled more obviously now, watching for the moment of realisation.

'Alan!' Rick explained.

McNabb nodded. 'It looks like he did have a change of heart. Either that or he got left behind when the rest of them fled. Whatever his reasons, he came to me shortly after we got back. He gave me some useful info to take to the police.'

'How's it going with them?' Rick wasn't sure that he wanted his boss to go to prison, despite everything that had happened.

'They seem happy that I'm cooperating. I don't think Nathan and the rest will be able to run forever. As for the future of the Mercury Group and Gold Force...' He shrugged. 'It's more a case of when than if.'

There was silence for a few seconds whilst Rick considered what would happen to everyone who worked for Gold Force.

'As far as the exit interview is concerned, I know that you're not going to be disappointed to leave and I wish you all the best for the future. You'll get a good reference. I advise you use it quickly before the world finds out what happened here.'

'Don't worry, I've already started looking,' Rick said. He signed a couple of forms and left the office.

By then, everyone was having a team meeting led by Dylan and most of them had their backs to Rick as he left. Dylan's speech slowed a little as he watched Rick walk through the door, and Rick turned and made eye contact for a second. Dylan half-smiled at him and Rick half-smiled back.

It seemed to Rick that his old team leader wasn't furious with him. Maybe McNabb hadn't told him what he'd lost out on. Either way, Dylan returned confidently to his speech whilst everyone in the room hung on his every word.

As he walked out of the main entrance, Rick knew that he would never have to enter the building again. He started speed-walking across the road and broke into a run as a white van going over the speed limit nearly flattened him. At the other side, he carried on running and didn't stop until he'd reached the bus station.

Thirty-one

Rick emerged from a pathway that was overhung with trees. As he pushed the branches out of the way, he saw an expanse of grassland before him. The location was perfect. He'd spent the last hour clambering up the steep hillside, occasionally deviating from the path to get a better view of the countryside behind him.

It was early summer and the day had been hot. Midges swarmed around Rick's sweat-soaked neck and his partially-bare legs. As he moved onto the open ground, he started what he had trekked all the way to the Peak District to begin.

His legs picked up speed and he started to sprint. The cobbles of the path gave way to undulating grass; the uneven fall of the land under Rick's feet felt far more satisfying than the constancy of tarmac and paving flags.

He didn't have long until he had to catch his bus home and he wanted to make the most of his time in the National Park. He ran wildly across the empty land. He hadn't seen another soul in over an hour, not since the dog walker and her poodle with its ridiculous full body Afro.

Running through the longer grass, Rick felt the reeds tickling his legs and pushed himself harder. Exercise no longer felt like a punishment, or a means to escape a stabbing, but a great physical liberation.

It was three months since he had left Gold Force and he was still unemployed. The money McNabb had given him was useful, but he knew it wouldn't last him much longer. For now, he would forget that and just run.

9 781914 083402